The O'Maras

Go Greek

The Irish Guesthouse on the Green series, Book 14

Michelle Vernal

Chapter One

♥

Maureen O'Mara smiled with the satisfaction of a job well done as her eyes grazed over the gleaming surfaces upon which her dust-free knick-knacks were carefully placed. She was standing in a patch of sunlight, one foot in the kitchen and one foot in her open-plan living room, with a well-earned cup of tea. Lemony Pledge scented the air because Wednesday was her dusting day. She liked giving the place a good going over while Donal played bowls.

Maureen had been the one to introduce him to the bowling club. But, unfortunately, it had swiftly become apparent that while they were compatible in most aspects of life, they weren't when it came to competitive situations like playing bowls. Living with your manfriend was all about compromise, so she'd gracefully opted to bow out of the club as her plate was full enough these days with her grandchildren and the activities she juggled between seeing them. On top of which, she was pleased Donal was getting to know some of the Howth locals. Besides, they didn't need to be joined at the hip. She didn't want them to become like Rosemary Farrell and Cathal Carrick the Cobbler, who were never out of one another's sight these days. It was very annoying when she was trying to converse with Rosemary, and Cathal was continually putting his penny's worth in.

There'd been an incident at Carrick's shoe shop just last month. Word had spread swiftly amongst the line dancing girls that if the closed sign was displayed in the shop window, you should not try the door handle just in case Cathal forgot to turn it over in the morning. Poor Agnes Doody had only wanted to chat about a pair of custom-made cowgirl boots because she was struggling to find a pair to fit around her bunions. Agnes refused to say what she'd seen barrelling into the shop. Still, and all there was a clue to be gleaned in the way she turned puce whenever she glanced Rosemary Farrell's way.

On Wednesday, Maureen didn't look after the toddler Kiera either. Tom's mam did the honours. All of this mattered because the dusting was not something to be attempted when either Donal or Kiera was about. This was because they'd both want to help, with disastrous results. Donal, bless his heart liked to do his fair share, but he could be cackhanded and was best left to the hoovering and changing of the sheets. As for Kiera's habit of banging whatever she'd got her chubby little hands on against the carpet like it was a drumstick she was after holding, well, say no more. Far too many memories were attached to her bits and bobs to let that pair loose with a duster. Speaking of which, Maureen's eyes flitted to the wooden canoe she'd carved in Vietnam, standing erect and proud on the sideboard. A work of art that was, if she did say so herself.

Housework was a thankless task, and she firmly believed in giving yourself a pat on the back for a job well done once it had been tackled. And it was imperative to reward oneself with a chocolate-coated digestive biscuit. But, unfortunately, the biscuit presently tucked in on the saucer had begun to melt against the side of the cup. So she crossed the floor to the French doors intending to fling them open and enjoy her morning break in the sunshine. 'There's a sea view to be admired, so there is Pooh,' she said to the oblivious poodle snoring on his doggy bed.

At that moment, however, the telephone rang. Maureen, always up for a chat, did an about-turn, padding toward the kitchen to answer it, pausing to set her cup and saucer on the table.

'Patrick!' She exclaimed delightedly, having been greeted by her firstborn's voice. 'How're things over there in Los Angeles? Which film stars have you seen out and about lately?' She pulled out a chair and sank down in it, preparing for a lovely mother/son catch-up. There'd be no mention of beaches and weddings on her part because Maureen prided herself on knowing all her children inside out. Although they were as different as the four seasons, they had one trait in common—digging their heels in if she were to make a fuss. So, the less said about Patrick and Cindy's ridiculous idea of getting married on an island instead of under God's roof, the better. Besides, why Patrick would entertain going barefoot on the sand on the most important day of his life was beyond her. His feet had never been his best feature, having been blessed with his father's big toes, which were best kept inside a sturdy pair of shoes, thanks very much.

Oh yes, Maureen thought, waiting for his reply as she peeled her biscuit off the cup and quickly chomped it down. You had to be cunning when it came to your children. At least, he'd not be saying his vows for a good while yet, so there was plenty of time to work on him. She knew convincing him to talk Cindy around to a Catholic Nuptial Mass wedding service would require subtlety, and she could be very subtle when the need arose. Ask anyone who knew her. Subtlety was her middle name.

'Grand Mammy. I've not seen anyone you'd have heard of recently. Daniel Day-Lewis isn't filming over here just now. How's yourself and Donal?' Patrick's voice pulled her back from her thoughts.

Maureen swallowed the remains of her digestive biscuit, feeling it scrape her throat on the way down. 'Oh, we can't complain, son. The sun's shining. Although, since you asked, my knees are paining me when I wake up, and Donal's back has been playing up. It's a little better since he's been going to see a masseuse, and he's taken himself off to the bowls this morning, so it can't be too bad.' Maureen remembered her youngest daughter's smart remark upon hearing Donal was after getting a massage and hastily added. 'She's a properly qualified masseuse he's been going to see. Rita specialises in the backs so she does, and she's not one of those ones whose hands slip like your sister was after insinuating.'

'Moira?'

'Moira.' Maureen confirmed lips compressed. Aisling had been given a look, too, for encouraging her, and as for those two sons-in-law of hers who were thick as thieves these days with their marathon plans, they should know better. She had a quick sip of her tea, noticing the packet of photos she'd picked up from the pharmacy yesterday was still on the table. She and Donal had flicked through them last night after dinner, agreeing there were some lovely snaps worthy of reprinting. 'I'm putting some photographs in the post for you of the reunion, so keep your eye out for them, Pat.'

'I will do, Mammy.'

Patrick's voice was tight, and if Maureen were a dog, her nose would have started twitching like Pooh's did when he was dreaming. Only this wasn't a dream; she was wide awake and could sense her son hadn't telephoned to catch up with family news. She gripped the phone with white knuckles. 'Come on then, son, out with it.'

'Hi, Mom!'

Maureen blanched at the breathy voice of her future daughter-in-law's voice twanging down the line.

'We'll tell her together, Pat.'

'Tell me what?'

'Cindy and I are bringing the wedding date forward, Mam,' Patrick blurted. Still, there was an underlying hint of sheepishness in his tone that didn't escape his mammy's notice.

Maureen stiffened. 'Why's that then?' She wasn't silly. The only thing left to tell, given they were already engaged, was that Cindy's personal care modelling days were ending, and she'd be moving into the maternity line of the fashion world.

'You're going to be a nan again, Mam,' Patrick said with the giddy excitement he used to get on Christmas morning as a boy.

'Congratulations, Grandma!' Cindy gushed.

She'd guessed right! She would be a nana again because her baby boy was to be a father himself! Maureen dropped the phone on the table with a clatter to clap her hands in delight. Where was Donal when she needed him? He should be here sharing in her excitement. She retrieved the phone and told her son and the soon-to-be mother of another precious grandchild she was over the moon at their happy news. 'Donal will be too, and your sisters. You've not told them yet, have you?'

'No, Mom/Mam. You're the first to know.' Cindy and Patrick were perfectly synced like Captain and Tennille.

'Very good. And how are you keeping Cindy?'

Ten minutes later, Maureen debated putting the phone on the table and making herself a fresh cuppa, having drained the last one. She doubted Cindy would notice as she gushed on about her first trimester. A simple 'everything's grand' would have done nicely. The tea would have to wait, though, because Patrick was back on the line telling Cindy she needed to conserve her energy and to go and put her feet up.

'You'll make a lovely Daddy and Cindy a grand little mammy,' Maureen sniffed through the happy tears that had welled hearing her son fussing about like so. 'Do you have one of those scan pictures like your sisters were after getting?'

'We do, Mammy. We'll email it to you.'

'You're not after having any more photographs taken, are you?' She'd yet to recover from the shot on the wall of Patrick and Cindy's apartment in Los Angeles. Pat insisted it was arty. Maureen thought it was porn.

'Not yet, Mammy, we thought we'd wait until Cindy was showing more and get some tasteful mammy-to-be photographs taken then.'

God help us all. Maureen raised her eyes heavenward but refrained from pass-remarking as she moved on to her next question. 'You didn't find out what you're having, did you?'

'It's too soon for that, Mammy, but Cindy's convinced it's a girl.'

'A girl would be lovely.'

'Or it could be a boy.'

'Indeed, Pat.'

'Er, Mammy, about moving the wedding date forward.'

'Yes, son?' Maureen thought that she'd have to work fast on the church thing, doing the maths and coming up with Novemberish being the baby's due date. Father Fitzpatrick would squeeze them in at Saint Theresa's though given he'd known all the O'Mara children since they were babies. A frisson of pride rippled through her because her son wouldn't be modern and have the baby attend his or her mammy and daddy's wedding. Cindy would be Cindy O'Mara before their little babby was born. That was a blessing and would earn brownie points with the good Father.

'The thing is it's all booked like. We're getting married on the Greek island of Santorini this September. But don't panic, Mammy, because it's nearly two months away.'

***

When Donal breezed in the door victorious after his bowls session, he found Maureen prone on the sofa with a flannel pressed to her forehead.

Chapter Two

♥

Nearly two months later

The seatbelt sign pinged off, and Donal shot out of his seat like a rocket and began rummaging about in the overhead locker to retrieve their carry-on bags, eager for the off. He passed Maureen's bag down to her. At the same time, she manoeuvred across his empty seat to squeeze into the aisle behind him with Leonard Walsh, shuffling across from the window seat he'd occupied, having to wait his turn to be able to stand up.

Aisling and Quinn were up the front of the plane in the bulkhead seats with the twins. From the sound effects that had drifted toward Maureen from the moment of take-off, they'd not had a pleasant flight and would be equally eager to get off the plane. 'Islands in the Stream' didn't have the same effect on little Aoife and Connor, so there'd been no point in herself and Donal venturing up the aisle to sing the duet. *They were quiet now, though, bless,* she thought, straining to catch their familiar cries above the hubbub of chatter and failing. As for Moira,

Tom, the toddler Kiera and Bronagh, they'd been seated in the row behind herself.

It had been Bronagh who'd kept Maureen sane in the whirlwind leading up to this trip to Greece. O'Mara's receptionist had a good head on her shoulders in a crisis.

Maureen jiggled from leg to leg to get her circulation going and shifted her bag so it wasn't digging into her shoulder. How tall people got on wedged in their seats for hours on end was a mystery. If they were animals, there'd be activists with placards out on the tarmac claiming cruelty. Her thoughts turned back to Bronagh as she twisted her neck and saw her friend was still in the window seat, waiting for the exodus to begin.

Bronagh Hanrahan had worked at O'Mara's guesthouse for so long that she was also part of the family. Maureen considered her a close confidante too. Not once had Bronagh flapped over the short notice of hers and her manfriend Leonard's wedding invitation, and upon seeing the state Maureen was in over all the arrangements that needed to be made to get her family to Patrick and Cindy's wedding, she took her old friend in hand and took charge.

It was Bronagh who'd booked the flights and accommodation for their week on Santorini and, in doing so, had steered Maureen through the choppy pre-wedding arrangement seas to the calm Aegean Sea waiting for them outside this aircraft. Her organisational skills were second to none, and it hadn't been a bother, Bronagh had said, handing over the portfolio of tickets with a beatific smile.

As for Roisin, Shay, and Noah, this week away couldn't have come at a better or worse time. Better in so much as poor Rosi and Shay were exhausted from all the upheaval of packing up hers and Noah's life in London to move back to Ireland. Howth, to be exact, and to say Maureen was delighted with this new arrangement would be an understatement. She and Shay had found a grand little place a stone's throw from the school Noah would be attending. Worse, they'd barely had time to unpack and settle into their new home before they were winging their way to Greece.

Still and all, Noah was very excited about being his Uncle Patrick and Aunty Cindy's ring-bearer. The responsibility of his role at the wedding had proved a good distraction from all the changes around him. They were big changes for a little lad to grapple with because it wasn't just that his mammy was moving them across the sea. They'd be living with Shay, too, after having been just him and his mammy this last while. Maureen was grateful for all their sakes that Noah thought the world of Shay still and all he wasn't his father. He had a father, and that eejit had accepted a job offer in Dubai which meant he'd not be there for his son anywhere near as much. That broke her heart.

Life had a funny way of sorting itself out, though, because, sure, hadn't Colin's decision to relocate to the Emirates meant Roisin had decided to come home to Ireland. Every cloud had a silver lining and all that.

Her grandson, bless him, seemed to be taking it all in his stride. Once Rosemary Farrell had agreed to look after Mr Nibbles and Stef, his pet gerbils, in his absence, he'd been excited about his important role and a week of sunshine and swimming before he started his new school. They were very adaptable young children, and Maureen hoped Noah would soon make some lovely new friends. Mind if things went to plan one day soon, he might have a little brother or sister.

Maureen was jostled from behind as Tom hefted all the paraphernalia down that Moira had insisted Kiera might need and hadn't touched for the four-and-a-half-hour flight.

'Sorry, Maureen.'

'Not a bother.' She'd a soft spot for all the fellas her daughters had wound up with. They were good men with the patience of Job to take on her girls. Sometimes she had to pinch herself at all that had happened these last few years. For a while, after her husband Brian had passed, she'd thought she'd never be happy again, but happy she was. Brian would be, too, from his vantage point upstairs, watching over them all.

Maureen had decided to pay for her children, their respective partners and grandchildren to attend Patrick and Cindy's wedding. It was what Brian would have wanted, and she couldn't be doing with listening to Moira prattling on about being a student and, as such, being unable to afford luxuries like weddings on a Greek Island. The line had been drawn at Kiera having her own seat, though. She'd regretted this decision after the tenth time Kiera had smacked her on the head, thoroughly enjoying herself standing on her mammy and daddy's laps. There'd been a five-minute reprieve when they'd hit turbulence, and she'd had to be buckled in, but sadly it hadn't lasted.

Brian would also be pleased with the contribution she'd gifted to Patrick and Cindy for the wedding in his memory because once she'd moved on from her pique at the service not being a proper Catholic one in a church, she'd felt it the right thing to do. Moira's foghorn voice broke her reverie.

'Was that you, Tom?' she was demanding.

'It was not. It's Kiera. I told you not to give her the apple.'

'Like father like daughter.'

Tempers were fraying, Maureen thought, wishing they'd get on with whatever they were doing up the front and open the door. Janey Mack, it was like standing in a mosh pit at a concert! Rod Stewart, sometime in the seventies, sprang to mind. What was the hold up? Maureen stood on ballerina toes to peer over Donal's shoulder. There was nothing to see, but a few seconds later, she exhaled her relief as they shuffled forward. Finally, she could see the two flight attendants in their smart blue Ryan Air uniforms nodding and smiling at the disembarking passengers.

Donal smiled at the attendants, already having assured them he wasn't Kenny Rogers earlier in the flight. "Twas a grand flight,' he beamed. Then it was Maureen's turn.

Up close, she could see the young girl on the left had trowelled on the makeup. If she was her mammy, she'd be telling her to go and wash some of that muck off her face. You didn't need all that slap on at her age. But she wasn't her mammy. She'd three girls of her own who were more than enough to deal with, thanks very much, besides which there was something more pressing to be dealt with.

'A word of advice to yourself and your Ryan Air wans.' Maureen looked from one attendant to the other. 'A cup of tea would have been nice.'

The foghorn blared behind her once more. 'It's a budget airline, Mammy. So if you want a cup of tea, you have to pay for it. I told you that earlier.'

However, Maureen had said her piece, and she trotted after Donal down the stairs to the blackened tarmac. The air was a warm caress, and a sea of stars danced above their heads. Tilting her head skyward for a moment, Maureen could see why the night sky fascinated the ancient Greeks. It was beautiful.

This was her first time standing on Greek soil, and while it hadn't been her choice as a destination for her only son's wedding, the idea had grown on her once Bronagh had come to the rescue. Of course, the added bonus of showing Rosemary Farrell the wedding photographs had softened her angst over Father Fitzpatrick's disapproval at the wedding being held on foreign soil and on the beach. As for who was officiating the service, Patrick had been cagey, and she'd yet to get a straight answer out of him. But, she'd not dwell on that now, not when they'd tired babbies needing their cots.

'Here they come,' Donal said, pointing to the stairs leading down from the plane. Maureen glanced back to see Tom staggering forth, laden with the bags they'd somehow been allowed to take on board. Moira, meanwhile, was on the top step trying to pick a protesting Kiera up. It was a battle of wills, and Maureen had a little grin seeing Kiera win as her mammy took her firmly by the hand and let her attempt the stairs. She was glad she couldn't overhear what the passengers waiting to disembark behind them were saying. Kiera gave up halfway down, and Moira swinging her onto her hip, hurried over to join Donal, Maureen and Tom to wait for Roisin, Noah and Shay. Bronagh and Leonard headed off to the terminal building in the wake of Aisling, Quinn and the twins. No doubt Aisling was prattling on about Connor and Aoife's routines being disrupted by the time difference. Santorini was two hours ahead of Ireland. The girl was obsessed with her babbies' routines.

Moira was after telling her how they'd gone to the swimming pool way over the other side of town because they were barred from the Aquatic Centre they'd gone to with Mammy and Rosemary Farrell. Aisling was doing a mother-and-baby session while Moira was getting pummelled with water by Kiera in the toddler group. According to Moira, her sister was only in the water five minutes before announcing she'd have to leave because it was the twins' sleepy time, and their routine couldn't be deviated from. So she'd ordered her sister out of the water and said they'd have to get on the road because the car's motion would lull them to sleep.

Who'd have thought women had been having babbies since the arrival of Adam and Eve?

The trickle of travellers continued to exit the plane until Roisin, Shay, and Noah appeared, waving down at them like they were descending Airforce One.

At last, the little group was gathered, and like moths to the flame, they headed toward the light.

Chapter Three

T he twins were sound asleep in their baby carriers, having worn themselves out. Thus, proving they were more adaptable than their mammy gave them credit for. Meanwhile, their frazzled parents flashed their passports at the Greek customs man. Maureen made a beeline for the shortest queue, and the others followed her.

'We'll see you at the luggage carousel,' Quinn called over his shoulder as they breezed through.

It was a pleasant surprise to see the passport control line was moving swiftly, and Maureen turned to Donal. 'It's because we've come in on a late flight. Yer man up there's eager to get home to his bed.' She did a lunge or two in her Mo-pants as though warming up for the Dublin Marathon Tom and Quinn were so set on taking part in. Then, she directed Donal to stretch and bend like she was. 'It's not good at our age, all that sitting, Donal, at any age for that matter. And, you'd do well to stop glaring at me and join in,' she shot at Moira.

'Jaysus Mammy, it's the airport we're in, not the fecking gym. Would you stop?'

'Well, I'm not complaining if yer customs man is in a rush to get off home,' Donal chortled, nearly clocking Tom in the eye as he followed Maureen's arm circle instructions.

Maureen wasn't listening, though, as she lobbed back at her daughter, 'I'm telling you, Moira, my granddaughter's first sentence is going to include the bad 'f' word. She'll be barred from going to the playgroups, the rate you're going.' She made a final lunge as the line inched forward. 'The toddler Kiera will not win friends and influence people by saying "Pass me some fecking playdough," so think on.'

In no time, Donal was waved up to the booth, and Maureen watched as he handed the uniformed man, who seemed to be on automatic pilot, his passport. She wasn't surprised when the officer glanced at it and then back at Donal twice before stamping the page. She'd seen Donal's passport photograph, and he bore an uncanny resemblance to Grizzly Adams rather than Kenny Rogers in it.

Maureen approached the man with narrowed eyes as she sought his name badge. 'Good evening there, Yiannas. I'm Maureen O'Mara visiting your country for my son Patrick's wedding.'

Yiannas didn't smile as he took her little book and opened it.

'That's not a good likeness,' Maureen said, referring to the Cell Block H photo Yiannas was frowning at. She might look like she'd been posing for a mug shot, but it occurred to her then that she wasn't the one who'd been collared at Boots. It was Moira. 'Do you see the young woman standing there?' she pointed to Moira, who was waiting her turn.

Upon seeing Moira, Yiannas sat up straighter, forgetting Maureen's passport. He adjusted his uniform and checked his breath by puffing into his hand and sniffing. 'Demi Moore?' His raspy voice suggested he was fond of a cigarette or twenty.

'No, that's not Demi, but you're not the first to make that mistake. That woman there is my youngest child, Moira O'Mara. I've pointed her out to you because I wanted to tell you that Moira isn't a criminal. It was a misunderstanding at the Boots chemist over a pregnancy test that she forgot to pay for. And, it was at least two years ago now so it shouldn't show up on her record, but I wanted to mention it just in case like.'

Yiannas shook his head. This little Irish woman was mad, but against his better judgment, he waved her through.

Maureen wasn't finished, though and while she didn't like to point out the proverbial elephant or wart in the room, she felt it would be in Yiannas's best interests. *Tourism could take a nosedive with that growth on his finger*, she thought, leaning closer to the swarthy officer. 'Listen, Yiannas. Do you see the tall lad next to Moira?'

Yiannas nodded, keen to get the show on the road, or he'd be here all night.

'Well, now, he's Moira's partner and a trainee doctor. He'll tell you how to sort that wart, there.' Maureen was about to pat him reassuringly on the hand. Still, she thought better of it and gave him a smile instead, hoping to convey that his days of carrying the HPV virus were nearly over. Then she moved off to join Donal.

She breathed a sigh of relief when her daughter and granddaughter were officially admitted to the island a few minutes later.

'I put in a good word for you, Moira. You know, with your criminal record like.'

'What?'

'The Boots thing and it helped that your Tom's a doctor in waiting.'

'Mammy, that was a misunderstanding, is all. I don't have a record.' Moira frowned, barely paying attention because she was too busy mouthing 'Hurry up' at Tom, who was examining the custom officer's hand.

They watched while Tom conveyed his prognosis to a grave Yiannas.

'What did you say to him? Was it bad news?' Maureen asked when he joined them as Roisin and Noah commiserated with the Greek man sitting behind the counter.

'It's the dry ice he needs.' Tom supplied.

Maureen and Donal made a tutting sound having both been there and done that.

Roisin and Noah were permitted entry, followed by Shay. An over-tired Noah was in a state of agitated excitement over the size of Yiannis's wart. At the same time, Roisin, who'd suffered from a verruca as a child, had nothing but sympathy for him.

At last, Bronagh and Leonard who'd somehow wound up in the slowest moving queue shuffled through, and Donal moved them all along. 'Come on, Aisling and Quinn will be wondering what's happened to us.'

A small crowd had gathered around the luggage carousel, all eager to get their bags and move on to their respective hotels. However, there were no signs of any cases as the group hustled alongside Aisling and Quinn.

Aisling turned her attention to Maureen. 'Mammy just so you know, I'm very grateful to you for treating us like but I'll not be flying home. I'm taking a boat back to Ireland.' She looked from Aoife to Connor, angelic now in sleep, but they'd only given in when the plane bounced down the runway.

Quinn nodded but wasn't saying a word, unlike Moira.

'I'll join you.' She jigged Kiera, clinging Koala-like to her mammy's hip. She was sucking her thumb in a sure sign she was sleepy. 'Having this one clambering all over you for four and a half hours was no picnic. I hope it's not far to the hotel because she's about to crash and if we don't get her to a bed before she gets her second wind, it will be a nightmare,' she sniffed. 'I was born to fly first class me.'

'You were born at the Holles Street Hospital, so cop yourself on.' Maureen huffed. 'Have you any complaints you'd like to get off your chest while we're at it?' she aimed at Roisin.

'No, Mammy. We were grand. Noah had a lovely chat about Mr Nibbles and Stef with the lady beside him. I doubt she bargained on being an authority on the breeding habits of gerbils by the time she arrived in Greece.'

'Fecky brown-noser,' Aisling and Moira mumbled over at their sister.

Bronagh watched a quartet of burly military men clomp past before nervously turning to Leonard. 'What's going on, Lenny? Have you read anything about a coup happening? They can kick off very suddenly, you know. I read Shirley Conron's Savages, and I've no wish to spend my holiday hiding out in the hills.'

'It would be just our luck to have arrived during a military coup.' Aisling added.

'There's nothing to worry about, Moira, Bronagh. The airport here serves both holidaymakers and the military forces, that's all,' Donal informed her. He'd done his homework. 'And it's about a ten to fifteen minutes' drive to Fira where we're staying.'

'You missed your calling, Donal. You could have been a tour guide,' Roisin informed him, ignoring Noah tugging her arm to say he was hungry.

All conversation was suspended as the luggage carousel juddered into life, and a lone blue bag popped through the flaps. It made a solitary round before being joined by a colourful array of luggage.

There it is, 'Grab it, Quinn!' Aisling pointed at the case that just about needed a plane of its own. Given the strict weight requirements, how she'd scraped it past your check-in woman was beyond Maureen.

One by one, the crowd trickled off weary voices mingling with excitement at arriving here on the Greek island of Santorini.

'Where's yours then, Mam?' Aisling asked, looking around and seeing that everybody else seemed to have their bag. 'I don't think there's any more coming through.'

'Mo, I think we should go and enquire over there,' Donal pointed vaguely to the only other sign of life in the terminal.

Maureen's lips flattened. This did not bode well.

Chapter Four

♥

Georgios Kyrgios placed the empty plate in the deep stone sink and patted his middle with satisfaction. The generous helping of Kleftico, his English neighbour, Wendy, who ran Stanley's, the pension next door she'd named after her late husband, had dropped around for his dinner, was delicious. They were both widows and had fallen into the amiable habit of sharing their evening meal and taking turns cooking. Not tonight, though, because they had guests arriving and had been busy preparing the rooms in their respective pensions. Still, Wendy had presented him with a plate of one of his favourite dishes, saying she'd had to cook anyway.

He had his late wife, Ana, to thank for Wendy, having mastered the traditional Greek dinner he'd just enjoyed. Ana had taken it upon herself to give their neighbour Greek cooking lessons, and Wendy had been a quick learner. The lamb had fallen apart when his fork touched it tonight and melted in his mouth.

Ana had befriended the English woman when she'd first arrived some five or so years back now, green around the gills as to the rhythms of life on their island but determined to make a go of things. Georgios didn't know for sure, but he suspected Ana, knowing she would be leaving him soon, had asked Wendy to keep an eye on him and ensure he ate properly. It was a task that should have fallen to their daughter, Obelia, not their neighbour.

Technically speaking, Stanley's was the competition, and Wendy might have embraced Greek culture and cuisine, but she hadn't abandoned her homeland entirely because the full English breakfast offered next door was very popular! There were enough tourists to fill their pensions throughout the spring, summer and autumn months, though. He often thought they were like the ants in the old fable during those months working hard to ensure they survived the winter ahead. Life was like that here on the island of Santorini, where he'd always lived.

He'd come to know his neighbour well over their shared meals, and she'd told him about the farm her husband had run, while she offered bed and breakfast in their rambling farmhouse accommodation. She'd spoken of the farm's stone walls and how the fields contained within them were a kaleidoscope of green. The sheep they'd farmed with the black faces, white noses and curled horns had provided them with a good life, and her house was built of stone and had floors that creaked and a fire that roared in the winter months, much like Stanley's she'd said laughing. Wendy had the sort of laugh that was contagious, and so he'd laughed too. She also had a kind heart with an understanding of what it was to be lonely even though you were surrounded by people. He was grateful for her company each evening, even if she beat him at Rummy more often than not.

Loneliness and finding themselves alone in their middle years were the common denominator on which their friendship was formed. Losing her husband had seen Wendy pack up her life in England's North and move to the sunny climes of Santorini for a fresh start. She'd visited once on a rare holiday from the farm and had thought how wonderful it would be to live somewhere so exquisite, so serene.

It was a dream tinged with sadness that she now did so, she'd confided one night before slapping down her winning hand of four Queens.

Georgios found it hard to understand how she could leave her two sons behind, but Wendy said they were grown men who had their own lives to get on with. They could visit, she'd argued. And, they had but each only once and on separate occasions bringing their respective families with them. Upon learning he was widowed, both had treated him with suspicion. He'd marvelled at the selfishness of adult children who didn't wish to share their lives with their lonely parents yet resented their parents forming new friendships that weren't part of the world in which they'd grown up.

In winter, Wendy would return to England to see her grandchildren, only staying for a short while, conscious of not outstaying her welcome. The few weeks she was away would drag because even though he'd plenty of other friends on which to lean, it was her shoulder he missed.

There was no fresh start for him after Ana died. He would stay here in Karterados because a promise was made to be kept.

Georgios promised his beloved wife when she'd been pregnant with their only daughter, Obelia, that the pension would be the legacy they would pass on to her. So Kyrgios's Pension was where he would stay until he joined Ana.

Obelia might have made it clear she didn't want to take over the family business, but it would still be hers one day.

'Obelia,' he sighed her name out loud. His daughter's name meant pillar of strength, but with that strength came a stubborn streak. It would break Ana's heart if she knew Obelia had no plans to return to Santorini and keep the family name alive through the pension.

Georgios reached for the briki to brew the Greek coffee. He adored hearing the echoing memory of Ana's voice as she stressed the importance of using extra finely ground, roasted coffee beans.

'Mix them with cold water, Georgios, and then let them seep over a gentle heat until the liquid becomes frothy and close to boiling,' she would boss.

He liked to think she was keeping a watchful eye on him from heaven because the one time he had tried to hurry things along before the liquid appropriately thickened, he'd fumbled and dropped the pot. It had taken him twice as long in the end to make it, given he had to start over again, and so, he'd taken it as a sign from his wife not to do it again.

Ana would brew coffee for him to enjoy twice a day when she was alive. In the morning, it woke him up, and in the evening, it allowed him to wind down and mull over the day. She'd done so since they were first wed when he was twenty-four and her a tender twenty-one.

Oh, what a beautiful bride she'd been. His eyes misted as he placed the pot on the stove. Her waist had been so tiny he could fit his hands around it, and her hair a mane of tumbling curls the colour of the coffee she'd brew. He'd thought her even more beautiful when her waist thickened with age and her hair streaked grey. Her eyes had shone with new wisdom, which he'd relied upon. He missed how his wife would sit across from him at the table her father had hammered together with his two hands as a wedding present, her dark eyes flashing as she helped him put the world to rights.

Georgios glanced at his watch as he watched the briki, waiting for the right moment to remove it from the stove. If the plane from Ireland was on time, it would land in a quarter of an hour. This would give him enough time to enjoy his coffee before he collected his and Wendy's guests. It was a group family booking that they'd split between them, and he'd pick them up from the airport in his van.

The froth was beginning to form, and waiting a few seconds more, he picked the briki off the stove and poured his cup. The froth was meant to be shared between cups, and sometimes Wendy would join him, pulling a face as she sipped at hers but determined to get used to the potent brew—it had been five years! Finally, he sat at the table, placing his cup in front of him before taking a contemplative sip.

Ana was an organised woman who'd run a tight ship regarding their business. They'd joke that she was the brains and he was the brawn. As for Obelia, well, she was their baby and their world. Obelia was enough; they'd reassure themselves as their dreams of the brothers and sisters that would follow her faded away. With her future in mind, Georgios and Ana had toiled long and hard from late March to September, each year catering to the whims of their guests. When the tourists vanished, leaving only a hardy few lingering, he'd take whatever odd jobs he could find, and Ana would give English lessons. Any extra money they made was ploughed into the pension's upkeep. It was Obelia's inheritance, after all.

When Ana's cancer came three years ago, it swept swiftly through her, taking his wife, Obelia's *mána*, from them. However, not before she had taught him and Wendy, it transpired everything she deemed necessary, including how to make good Greek coffee.

'You must do it all now, my darling Georgios. At least until Obelia has finished her studies and comes home,' Ana had asserted, with the speckling perspiration along her hairline and strain in her voice the only signs she was in pain. He knew she took comfort in knowing she wouldn't be leaving him all alone because he'd have Obelia and the friendship of Wendy next door. Georgios held her small workworn hands in his, unable to imagine his life without her.

Ana would be turning in her grave if she knew how it had all worked out. How he'd not seen his daughter in over two years and that he'd pick up the phone planning to talk through the mess they'd made of things only to put it down once more. He'd thought he wouldn't ever have to feel the pain of loss so acutely again after Ana's death. But then Obelia had shattered his heart all over again.

Perhaps Ana did know, he thought, raising tired brown eyes toward the ceiling and wishing he hadn't as he spied a crack. Filling it was another task to add to his never-ending to-do list. The walls also needed a fresh coat of paint in here, but that was a job for winter.

The kitchen wasn't a grand room, but it was a room that used to be filled with laughter and love. These days he could hear himself breathing when he sat in it, lost in his memories when Wendy was away or hadn't joined him to eat.

The telephone in the hall shrilled an incoming call, and he swiftly drained his cup and got up to answer it.

Their Irish visitors must have arrived.

Chapter Five

Maureen opened the curtains to greet the day while Donal's snores rumbled from the bed, where a single white cotton sheet covered his slumbering form.

'Sweet Mother of Divine, Donal wake up, would you? I've never seen a sky so blue. And you want to see the pool. It's sparkling in the sun. I can't wait to take a dip!'

A snorty snore sounded, and Maureen dragged her eyes away from the vista and crossed the floor to the bed, feeling the tiles smooth and cool beneath her bare feet. She decided there was nothing for it but to give him a good shake, eager to venture downstairs for breakfast and begin the day. They'd a lot to be getting on with, meeting Patrick and Cindy at their villa being top of the agenda after a quick swim mind. So, leaning over the bed, she shook Donal with considerable vigour before stepping back.

Donal's eyes flew open, 'Earthquake!' His bleary-eyed gaze was pan- icked as he tossed the sheet aside and stood to attention. 'Take cover, Mo.'

'No, you eejit, it was me giving you a shake,' Maureen said as he registered her standing there. She shook her head, and her freshly highlighted hair swished back and forth, grazing her shoulders. 'Did

I not tell you to stop reading that book you got out of the library?'
Donal had been glued to a pictorial hardback called The Santorini
Caldera in the weeks leading up to their trip. He'd been like a cuckoo
poking his head out of it repeatedly to read out earthquake statistics.
He'd also taken to calling the island Thira, which Maureen rather liked
because it made him sound like some sort of professor.

Rosemary Farrell's nose had been put out of joint when she'd explained Santorini had been known as this since ancient Greek times.
Her manfriend might be a mover and shaker in shoe cobbling, but
he couldn't spout facts like that. Maureen thought a trivial pursuit
evening with Rosemary and Cathal might be in order once they got
home. She'd also enjoyed dropping around Howth that her eldest and
only son, Patrick, was marrying a supermodel (technically, she was
when it came to the world of personal hygiene television adverts) on
the island of Thira. Although she'd noticed the line dancing ladies'
eyes had glazed over when she'd mentioned this again last Tuesday.
However, she hadn't been impressed with the late fine Donal had
incurred when he'd returned the Santorini book to the library the day
before yesterday. She'd told him he should have asked the librarian for
a special dispensation on account of having a wedding to attend on the
Greek Island. You had to be proactive in this world, she'd said with a
tut.

'Mo, you gave me a start there.' Donal said, scratching his beard.

'Sorry Donal, but you can't be sleeping the day away, not when
there's a view outside that window there that has to be shared, and
we've got a million and one things to be getting on with.'

They'd arrived here at the Kyrgios's Pension under darkness last
night, and their party had been split. Aisling, Quinn and the twins,
Bronagh and Leonard, were to stay next door at Stanley's. Maureen
had thought Stanley's didn't have a very Greek ring to it. While she,

Donal, Moira and Tom, Roisin and co were staying here. Their host
Georgios, who'd picked them up from the airport, had chatted away
to his weary charges in accented English about all the things they'd
find to do on his magnificent island as they bumped down narrow
streets toward the village of Karterados. Maureen had to interrupt him
because they weren't here solely to sightsee. They were here for her
son's wedding to an American supermodel who was with child.

Georgios, who'd been suitably impressed by Maureen's revelation,
had delivered the foursome staying at Stanley's to their host, Wendy.
Wendy didn't sound very Greek to Maureen's ears either. Georgios
carried their luggage inside Stanley's with the help of Quinn and
Leonard before ushering the rest of them through his front door. He'd
welcomed them with a glass of fresh juice in the reception area before
pointing out where breakfast would be served between eight and ten
o'clock. Then, he'd helped them lug their bags up the stairs to their
rooms.

Maureen's practised eye had determined her and Donal's double
room, while hardly ornate with its simple furnishings, was clean and
functional. She particularly liked the sunset print on the wall. It was
very eye-catching.

'You are happy?' Georgios asked from where he stood in the hallway.

'It will do nicely, thank you, Georgios.' Maureen smiled at the
deeply tanned man with a shock of dark hair, greying about the temples. He had a moustache and was putting her in mind of Tom Conti
in Shirley Valentine. She knew one or two of her line-dancing ladies,
Bold Brenda in particular, would be more than happy to head out on
his boat with him if he invited them.

'I will see you at breakfast then. And I will telephone the airline to
see if they've located your suitcase in the morning. Good night.'

'Good night, Georgios,' Donal called from where he was checking out the tea-making facilities.

'Thanks a million. Good night, Georgios.' Maureen closed the door with his promise ringing in her ears.

Donal was already filling the kettle. She'd kicked off her shoes and propped cushions up behind her back before stretching out on the bed. Donal carried their hot drinks over, and they'd sat sipping the brew in between, talking in hushed voices about how exciting it would be to wake up somewhere different in the morning.

Now here they were, and Donal followed Maureen's lead, creaking and groaning as he did so. 'That bed was like a rock,' he grumbled, joining her at the window. His back was forgotten, though, as blinking against the brightness, he soaked in the pool and cloudless sky above it. 'That's a sight for sore eyes, so it is.'

The pension they could see in the light of day was a white L-shaped building, and they were staying in the wing closest to the street with Roisin, Shay and Noah in the room next door. Moira, Tom and Kiera's room was in the shorter part of the 'L' above the guests' dining area, separated from the courtyard by an archway. Georgios's living quarters were also downstairs.

Cobalt blue shutters framed all the windows, and a bougainvillea spilt over the top of the wall opposite Maureen and Donal's room, separating them from Stanley's in a glorious riot of purple flowers. The courtyard below was dominated by the pool around which sun loungers, shaded by blue umbrellas, were laid out in invitation. A spiky plant in a terracotta pot stood guard in the far corner.

Maureen could hear the distant whine of scooters zipping about the place and the sounds of village life outside their pension. Closer to home was the clink of cutlery as Georgios, she guessed given he'd told her he ran the accommodation single-handed, laid the tables in readiness for breakfast. Her stomach rumbled in anticipation, and she was set to turn away from the window when she caught movement out of the corner of her eye.

The curtains that had been closed across the way were now open, and Maureen shaded her eyes to see Moira with Kiera on her hip, looking back at her. She waved vigorously and chirped, 'Calamari, Moira, Kiera!'

'It's Kalameri, Mo. That's good morning or good day in Greek.'

'Donal, that's what I said.'

Moira placed her hand over her daughter's eyes. 'Jaysus wept! Don't be waving like that until you've your bra on, Mammy. Is that Donal's tee shirt you're after wearing? And Donal, what are you thinking? It's not decent standing in windows wearing just your underpants. You're hurting my eyes, so.'

The fact that Moira's tee shirt barely covered her arse was neither here nor there.

Donal fled while Maureen remembered her dilemma and informed her daughter, 'I'll have to make my way around to your room. I'll be there in a few minutes.'

'Why? You've your own room. What's wrong with that?'

'She's always a mardy madam in the mornings before her coffee, Donal,' Maureen flung over her shoulder before turning back to the window. 'To borrow some clothes, that's why. My poor suitcase is likely gallivanting around the African continent for all I know.'

'Don't waste your time Mammy. I've nothing that will fit you,' was tossed back.

'You do, too. There's that lovely pink sundress with white polka dots. I like a polka dot, and it would look well on me. Sure, I'd get that dress over my head, not a bother.'

'No, Mammy, you're not to be stretching the booby part. Why can't you wear what you wore on the plane yesterday? Your case should be here before lunchtime.'

'Moira, would you use the brains God gave you? Sure, look at that sky and the big golden thing in it. Any eejit can see it's too hot for long sleeves and Mo-pants. The pink sundress will do nicely, thank you, and I'll be borrowing some clean knickers while I'm at it. Those bits of floss things you wear are a one size fits all. They must be given you could use them as a slingshot.'

'You're not wearing the dress, Mammy, and you'd do yourself an injury if you tried to wear my knickers. Try Aisling. She'll have a tent dress and a pair of parachute panties for you to pilfer.'

Maureen's eyes narrowed as her youngest child wrenched the curtain closed, signalling the end of the conversation. She huffed silently, debating going around there and demanding her daughter hand the dress and clean floss-like knickers over. The ungratefulness of her! And after she'd been treated to a week in the sun. 'Donal, did you hear how she's after speaking to me?'

'Me and half of Thira, Mo, my love.' Donal replied, towel slung over his arm in readiness for a shower.

'She's lungs on her stronger than that Maria Callas wan had. It's a shame she can't hold a tune,' Maureen grumbled. 'I'll tap on Rosi's door and see what she brought that I can borrow.'

'You do that.' Donal said, blowing her a kiss. 'The shower will be free by the time you get back.'

Maureen thought him a fine figure of a man indeed, and in her book, it had been a sign of true devotion him letting her use his toothbrush last night.

That Moira one didn't know she was born, she thought, blowing him a kiss back, her equilibrium restored.

Chapter Six

Maureen rapped on the door, and it swung open a split second later to reveal Noah wearing a snorkel mask. He was also clad in his O'Mara's Reunion tee shirt with swim shorts and flippers.

'Calamari, Noah.'

Noah cut straight to the chase. 'Nana, you've forgotten your trousers. Will you come downstairs with me so I can go for a swim, please?'

'Not until you've had your breakfast, Noah. I told you that.' Roisin said, raising her eyes from where she was sitting on the side of the bed about to put her shoes on. 'Let your Nana in the door now. She shouldn't be loitering about the place in just a tee shirt.'

Noah moved away from the door, and Maureen stepped inside. 'Why don't you go and knock on your Aunty Moira's door and play with Kiera until we're all ready to go down for our breakfast?'

'That's a good idea, Noah,' Roisin said.

'But I want to go for a swim.' His flippers slapped over the tiles to the chair by the window, and he flopped down in it.

Roisin sighed and began fastening the straps of her pretty sandals as Maureen closed the door behind her. The sound of running water signalled Shay was in the shower.

'Did you and Donal sleep well, Mammy?'

'Like logs, although Donal's after saying the bed wasn't much cop for his back.'

'Shay's after telling me Greek beds are always like rocks.'

'Ah, well, that's the price you pay for all that glorious sunshine out there.' Maureen got down to business. 'I've come to borrow something to wear until my suitcase arrives. I asked Moira, but she's after being very rude to me, so she is.'

Roisin grinned, 'That doesn't sound like Moira,' her tongue very much in her cheek as she stood up. 'I packed lightly, but let's see what I've got.' Her suitcase was open at the foot of the bed, revealing a jumble of clothes.

'Why've you not hung those up?'

'I'm on my holidays, Mammy. There's such a thing as island time. I'll do it later.'

Maureen tsked. 'I taught you better than that. Sure, what will your man, Georgios, think of me when he comes in to make your bed and sees you've not bothered to put your things in the wardrobe?'

Roisin ignored her and rifled through the colourful pile, pausing to hold up a pair of cut-off shorts, 'What about these?' She frowned, eyeing the waistband. 'I don't know if they'll fit you, though.'

'Don't be casting aspersions about my middle, Roisin. I'll let you know I've the waist of a young girl thanks to the cutting back Donal and I have been doing in readiness for the wedding.'

'A very big girl, Nana,' Noah said.

Maureen thought, *Out of the mouths of babes*, with a glower in his direction. 'Moira might let you have one of Kiera's rusks, Noah. Why don't you go and tap on their door?' Of course, her granddaughter no longer needed them, but they made an excellent alternative to her unsanitary habit of chewing on whoever's flip-flops she could get hold of. Moira usually had a rusk or two on her person, and Maureen was pleased when Noah, who was also partial to the hard-baked teething biscuits, hopped off the chair and slapped over to the door, opening it.

He made his way down the hall to his Aunty's door, and peeking around the door frame, Maureen waited until he'd disappeared inside the room before closing the door again. Then, she turned her attention back to the shorts. 'No, Roisin, I can't be wearing the raggedy shorts at my age.'

'Why not?'

'Have you no sense, child? I'd look like I can't afford the good shorts.'

Roisin put the shorts back with a shake of her head, and Maureen strode over to investigate the contents of the case herself.

'This is more like it.' She held up a white, floaty, one-shoulder dress.'

'Ah, no, Mammy, I haven't worn that yet. I bought it especially to wear out for dinner with Shay.'

'Well, I don't see the problem if you were planning to wear it in the evening. This tortoiseshell fastener at the shoulder is nifty.' Maureen hugged the dress against herself and struck a pose.

'But it won't have the same wow factor if you've already worn it.'

'I've the wow factor, thank you very much.'

'Mammy,' Roisin tried a different tack, 'can you not call over and see Aisling. Sure, she'll have something more suitable for you to borrow.'

'That's what your sister was after suggesting, and no, I can't because I don't want to traipse next door in nothing but a tee shirt.'

Roisin opened her mouth, but Maureen held her hand up to silence her. 'Before you say it, I'm not wearing yesterday's clothes. Besides, there's no need not when this dress is going begging. And,' Maureen kept a tight hold on the dress with one hand, her free hand beginning to rifle through the case once more, 'I'll need knickers too and a swimsuit if you've a spare.'

'Rosi,' Shay's voice boomed from the bathroom. 'Did I hear the door go? Has Noah gone next door?'

'He's gone to see Moira in the hope of cadging a rusk.' Roisin replied before trying to yank the lacy knickers her mammy had picked out off her. 'You're not wearing those!'

'I'm not wearing anything. So, why don't you join me?' The door to the bathroom was flung open, and Shay was standing there with a cloud of steam billowing out behind him in all his morning glory.

Roisin let go of her end of the knickers so quickly they acted like a slingshot pinging Maureen in the chest before shrieking, 'Close your eyes, Mammy!'

'Feck! Maureen. Sorry! Feck, I didn't know you were here,' Shay's hands made a poor attempt to cover his bits before he backed into the bathroom and banged the door shut.

Maureen dropped the dress and sank onto the end of the bed like a swooning maiden, closing her eyes as she recited one Hail Mary after another.

Rosi wasn't called Easy Osi Rosi for nothing. It didn't take her long to bounce back from the shock of her fiancé flashing her mammy, and deciding enough was enough, she said, 'It's not like you're the Virgin Mary. C'mon now, Mammy, pull yourself together. You've seen one todger, you've seen them all, like.'

'I'll remember that,' Shay's muffled voice sounded through the bathroom door.

Maureen paused mid-way through her fifth round of the prayer and opened her eyes, blinking rapidly. 'I've not seen one like that before, Roisin. Holy God above tonight, my eyes are watering so.' She stood up, tugging Donal's tee shirt down. 'Now listen to me carefully. You're to tell Shay we'll never speak of this moment again. It didn't happen, and when I leave this room, I will pretend I was never here.'

'Fine by me.'

'And me!' came the muffled voice once more. 'It never happened.'

There was a tap on the door.

'What now? I don't think my poor heart can stand much more.' Maureen rested her hand on her chest as she edged toward the door.

'There's nothing wrong with your heart, Mammy.'

Maureen ignored her, cautiously opening the door to find Donal standing there, a white cap on his head and a wide grin.

'I've good news, Mo. Your suitcase has arrived.'

Maureen recited five more Hail Marys for good measure.

Chapter Seven

'Jaysus, my back.' Tom hobbled Quasimodo-like into the dining room after Moira, who gestured for him to pull the high chair over as she commandeered a table.

'Stop your moaning. I offered to rub some Deep Heat in.' Moira turned to her mammy and Roisin crowding into the room behind her. 'He never leaves home without it. Aisling's after telling me Quinn's the same. I'll be glad when this Dublin Marathon's over and done with, so he'll stop smelling like a mentholated cough sweet.'

'Can you blame me for not letting you near me with the Deep Heat?' Tom said, lifting the tray on the high chair so Moira could sit Kiera down in it. 'Not after what happened.'

'What happened?' Maureen asked, moving to where the continental breakfast was laid for them. Her brown eyes swept the generous assortment of bread to be toasted with a bowl of spreads, a choice of cereal, yoghurt, fruit, muffins and cake, rolls and cold cuts of meat, and squares of cheese. There was a pot of dark, rich coffee or hot water for the tea and a jug of orange and apple juice.

'Never mind,' Tom said hastily.

Moira lowered her voice as she strapped Kiera in and addressed Roisin. 'He's had a few nasty incidents with the stuff but still insists on using it. Unfortunately, the last time I gave him a leg rub, I accidentally got the Deep Heat, where Deep Heat has no business going. I warned Aisling and Quinn to make sure they always wash their hands after using the stuff.'

Roisin grimaced, and the menfolk in the room, Tom included, shuddered.

'I'm not silly, you know, despite what you girls think. I know what you're on about. It's like the massages where the fingers slip only with the Deep Heat.'

'Mammy!' Roisin and Moira pealed in sync. 'There're children present.'

'What's a massage where the fingers slip, Nana?' Noah asked right on cue.

'Thanks a million, Mammy,' Roisin said before giving Noah a convoluted story about how when someone had an injury, sometimes having that injury rubbed helped, but there was always a danger of finger-slipping due to the oil applied to the skin. Her son had switched off by the time she reached the end.

'Well, I wouldn't mind a lend of the Deep Heat, Tom. My back's killing me, too,' Shay griped, pulling out a chair next to Roisin and sitting down. He looked everywhere but at Maureen, who was rifling through the various spreads on offer.

Donal wasn't to be left out. 'I might as well have slept rough like those poor souls with nothing but a piece of cardboard to call home. You could send some my way too, Tom.'

'Sure thing, both of youse. I'll pass it on after breakfast. Moira, would you please get me a coffee since you're up?' Tom groaned, easing himself down into a chair.

'Rosi, I need a strong dose of caffeine to sort me out,' Shay whimpered.

'Mo, the lads are right. Coffee is what the doctor ordered.' Donal sat down gingerly.

'I'll make them,' Maureen said with a hint of martyrdom. 'Girls, you sort the children with their breakfast.'

Roisin and Moira grabbed a bowl each from the stack, but Noah sprang up between them before they could fill them with cornflakes.

'Cake for breakfast!' He was already whipping the cloche cover off, plate in hand, ready to help himself.

Kiera banged her spoon excitedly like she was participating in a protest and shouted something close enough to cake for them all to get the gist.

'I don't know what you're so excited about, madam. It's the cereal you'll be having,' Moira tossed over her shoulder.

'You should be having cereal first, too, Noah. Set an example for your cousin.' Roisin slapped his hand away from the cake.

'Nana, can I have a piece of cake, please?' Noah ignored both his mother and aunt.

Maureen, who'd been thinking about Patrick and how good it would be to see him in a few short hours, replied, 'You're on your holidays. I don't know why not. Go for your life there, Noah.'

'I give up,' Roisin said, shrugging as her son loaded a piece of dark, cinnamon-dusted cake on his plate.

Moira knew there'd be murder if Kiera missed out. So she plated a piece of the cake for her and was relieved when her daughter stopped banging her spoon, intent on shovelling it all in her mouth.

'Is it the milk you're after having, Shay?' Maureen asked, eyes trained on the milk jug.

'A splash, thanks, Maureen.'

'Tom, one or two sugars?'

'Two, please, Maureen.'

Maureen tutted, 'I don't know, and you a doctor in waiting.'

Finally, she carted the various cups over to the seated men, still avoiding eye contact with Shay, who feigned interest in the salt shaker as she placed his syrupy brew in front of him. *This morning's incident might never have happened, but it would still take a day or two to forget the enormity of what she'd seen*, she thought, joining her daughters in filling plates.

It was only a short time before everyone was seated in the room, just big enough to accommodate them all. The pale blue tablecloths soon became decorated with crumbs as they tucked in.

Donal, Tom and Shay had perked up after their caffeine fix and were eating heartily in between telling war stories about hard beds they'd slept on in their time.

'So what's the plan, Mammy?' Moira asked before crunching into her toast. One eye was on the sparkling pool through the open French doors, the other ensuring Kiera didn't send the cereal bowl she'd moved on to flying.

Georgios appeared in the doorway, then greeted them with a bright and cheery, '*Kalimera* everyone. I trust you slept well.'

'Calamari Georgios. We slept like logs, didn't we?' Maureen eyeballed Donal, Tom and Shay.

'Yes, grand thanks.' Donal beamed.

'I slept as though floating on a cloud,' Tom added.

'It was like laying down on a bed of air.' Shay laid it on thickest, desperate for brownie points where Maureen was concerned.

'I have a message for you from your son, Patrick.' Georgios passed a note to Maureen, who read it out loud.

'We'll see you at our resort for lunch today at one o'clock.'

'But I want to go swimming!' Noah shouted through his mouthful.

Kiera began banging her spoon and shouting once more.

'We'll go for a swim once your breakfast has gone down. It's only nine o'clock. We've plenty of time before we need to go to Patrick and Cindy's hotel.' Maureen said, sharing Georgios' smile at the little ones' enthusiasm. 'It'll be great to see them. It's been too long since the whole family was together.' She wondered at the flicker of sadness that crossed Georgios face. Perhaps he was widowed because there was no sign of a Mrs Kyrgios. That was a sadness both she and Donal could relate to. She was sure there'd be time for a cosy chat with their host later. She'd get to the bottom of it then.

'There'll be time to wander around the village outside too,' Roisin informed her son, who was busy miming a doggy paddle, giving Kiera the giggles.

'You will be able to see our windmill and cave houses. They're very old.' Georgios directed at Noah.

Noah frowned. 'Is the windmill like the ones on the Teletubbies, and are the cave houses as old as Nana and Poppa D?'

Georgios looked bewildered, and Roisin laughed, 'No, it's not like the Teletubbies ones. They're turbines. This is a windmill, and don't be rude about your Nana and Poppa D. They're not old.'

Maureen moved the conversation along, 'My son and his bride-to-be are staying at the Azure Waters Suites and Spa, do you know it?' she asked Georgios.

Their Greek host gave a low whistle that stirred the bristles of his moustache, 'I do. It's very nice.'

'Is it close enough to walk there from here, Georgios?' Donal enquired.

Georgios shook his head. 'No. It is in Oia, which is too far on foot. There is a bus or taxi.' His eyes glimmered. 'Or if you are feeling adventurous, you could see a little of our island more traditionally. For example, I could drive you to the road between Imerovigli and Oia

Village and from there, you can ride a donkey up the old path to Oia? My dear friend Konstantinos runs a donkey ride business and gives a good discount to guests of Kyrgios's and Stanley's.'

'Mum, Mum! Can we?' Noah was jumping up and down in his seat.

There was more spoon-banging and shouting.

'Are the donkeys well treated?' Roisin asked.

'Like his own children.'

'It does sound like fun,' Roisin smiled at Shay, who didn't look as convinced, but Moira was already putting her hand up and saying, 'Yes, please' to Georgios. Maureen wasn't going to miss out, either.

'What sounds like fun?' Aisling crowded into the room. 'Quinn's coming over with the twins shortly. Wendy said you don't mind us using the pool too, Georgios?'

'Of course not. You are to feel free to come and go.'

'Thanks a million,' Aisling dimpled. 'Bronagh and Leonard have gone for a stroll around the village.'

'We'll do the same, but we thought we'd have a dip first,' Moira piped up. 'And then we've to be at Patrick and Cindy's luxury pad for lunch at one.'

'Grand.'

'Georgios here's after telling us we can get a donkey into Oia,' Maureen told her middle child.

Aisling stared at her mammy blankly.

Maureen shook her head. 'A donkey, Aisling. Stop looking so gormless. Sure, they've four legs, a tail, and they bray.' She peeled her lips back, revealing her gums and teeth before making a noise that was a cross between a pig's oink and a dog's bark.

Kiera burst into tears.

'Now look what you've done, Mammy,' Moira said. 'What were you thinking?'

'I wasn't thinking, I was braying.'

'I know what a donkey is, Mammy.' Aisling stated, taking a step toward the buffet table.

'Georgios didn't mean help yourself to the food on offer too, Aisling. Sure, you've just had your breakfast.'

'I'm breastfeeding twins, Georgios,' Aisling explained, gratified when he indicated she should help herself. And, with a scowl in her mammy's direction, she placed the last piece of cake on a plate. 'So g'won then and explain what's got you braying about the place like so, Mammy.'

Maureen elaborated on the finer points of the planned journey to the northern part of the Caldera.

'Quinn has a fear of donkeys, so he won't be joining you,' Aisling said, popping a piece of cake in her mouth.

'Why's he frightened of donkeys?'

'I don't know. He just is. What about the rest of you? Are you all going?' Aisling fixed on Tom, Donal and Shay.

Under normal circumstances, Shay, in the honeymoon phase of his engagement to Roisin, would willingly ride a donkey if it made her happy, but he couldn't face it. Not with his back paining him so. As for Tom and Donal, they knew who wore the underpants in their relationships, and it wasn't often they said no to their beloveds. Still, on this occasion, they bowed out.

'I can't see Leonard being keen, so we might as well make it a girls' outing to Oia.' Maureen stated. 'Bronagh won't want to miss the craic. Noah, you can be an honorary girl,' she added hastily, seeing her grandson's face fall.

'Other women have trips to the spa when they are on their hols. We get to ride an ass.' Moira mumbled.

'And you'll enjoy it, too.' Maureen glared from one daughter to the other. 'All three of you.'

Chapter Eight

♥

The village of Karterados was filled with traditional, white-washed cube buildings. A slash of the bluest sea Maureen or any of their group had ever seen could be glimpsed in the distance. Old men sat smoking and watching the world go by around the main square while cats lazed in the sun and women wearing black went about their business. A pink and white church with a blue domed roof provided a photo pitstop, and Noah counted six bells on its tower.

The small Irish ensemble had poked around the cave houses, admired the windmill, and was venturing back into the main square, with Donal and Maureen leading the way. Donal had appointed himself their unofficial tour guide, given he was a walking encyclopaedia on Santorini. He was also easy to spot with his white cap.

The air was warm but not unpleasant. If it hadn't been for the wintergreen and menthol pong of the ointment the male members of their party had slathered on after a boisterous swim in the pension's pool earlier, they'd have caught the delicious aroma of Greek pastries from the bakery they were passing.

'I think it's lovely how the little square buildings are all painted white and blue,' Maureen said dreamily, holding Noah's hand. 'Did you ever see anything so pretty? And the flowers! The colours are so bright they almost hurt my eyes.'

The little boy was licking the promised ice cream his mother had bribed him with in exchange for getting out of the pool earlier. He made no comment, too intent on the frozen vanilla treat.

Aisling and Roisin were strolling along the cobbles behind Maureen and Donal, and unlike her son, Roisin spoke up. 'It's like a picture postcard,' she murmured. 'Gorgeous.'

'That reminds me. I'll pick a couple of postcards up later and send them to Freya and everyone, as well as Alasdair and the rest of Quinn's crew,' Aisling said, more to remind herself to do so than anything. Freya was running O'Mara's in their absence while Alasdair was in charge of Quinn's, her husband's namesake bistro. She glanced over her shoulder, seeing Quinn bouncing the twins in the pram. The motion had seen them both fall asleep as he chatted to Shay and Tom, who had Kiera strapped to his back. Her plump little legs dangled from the backpack, and the sun hat Moira had picked up and placed firmly back on her daughter's head at least five times since they'd left the pension was now slipping down over one eye. As for Moira, she needed to catch up, having paused to check out sunglasses on a stand despite having a perfectly good pair holding her glossy dark hair back from her face perched on top of her head.

'Actually, ladies, the buildings are cubic and representative of Cycladic architecture,' Donal replied knowledgeably. 'There's a school of thought that the limewash exteriors are down to a cholera outbreak in the thirties. So the Greeks were ordered to paint their buildings with lime which has antibacterial properties to halt the spread of disease.'

It wasn't exactly a romantic explanation, but still and all, Maureen gazed at her live-in manfriend with pride. 'If you want to know anything about the island girls, just ask Donal. He's done a lot of reading up on it and was after telling me Santorini's made up of five islands with only two of them having anyone living on them, weren't you, Donal?'

'I was Mo. This island, Thira, is the largest.'

Maureen was no longer listening as she squinted at a couple a little ways ahead of them. Their faces were shaded by wide-brimmed sun hats as they wandered along hand in hand, and she clicked it was Bronagh and Leonard. 'Ahoy there!'

'Mammy, please don't say "Ahoy there" ever again.' Roisin cringed. 'Not even if we were on board a boat which we're obviously not.'

'Yes, please don't,' Aisling reiterated.

Having caught them up, Moira grasped hold of the tail end of the conversation, 'Mind you, we have Captain Stubbing at the helm.' She referenced Donal's cap.

The sisters giggled, and Aisling began humming the theme tune from 'The Love Boat,' an old TV show that had run from the late seventies to the eighties. They'd enjoyed watching it when they were small and the choice of television programmes limited.

Maureen, who wasn't contrite in the least, paid them no heed as she cupped her hands on either side of her mouth and hollered, 'C'mere to me now, Bronagh! We're after going on a donkey ride.'

***

Georgios waited patiently for his and Wendy's guests to settle in the back of his van, listening to their excited chatter. It made him proud to hear them speak of the beauty of his village. Its views over the verdant valley filled with vineyards and down to the eastern shores where clear, dark blue waters sluiced black volcanic pebbles up and down the beach were not as dramatic as those overlooking the Caldera from Fira and Oia. But nevertheless, they were breathtaking.

Their clamouring voices were a welcome distraction from the sadness that had made his bones ache this morning. The mother, Maureen's comment about her excitement over having her whole family together here on Thira, had seen him sitting at his kitchen table, staring into space once his guests had gone out. *What was Obelia doing right now?* he'd wondered. If Wendy were seated opposite him, she'd look at him with her earnest grey eyes and say, 'A penny for them.' He'd tell her what he was thinking, and she'd shake her head and tell him he was a stubborn fool who should pick up the telephone and simply ask his daughter how she was.

He had picked up the phone to call her numerous times. He'd even got so far as tapping out the first few digits, but then his index finger would rest on the following number and refuse to press it. Where did he start, and what would he say to her? How did he make something right that had gone so badly wrong? Wendy would tell him you could only begin to fix things by opening the lines of communication, and it was on him to do so. He'd disowned Obelia after all in a moment of heated anger, but stupid pride had him in a chokehold.

Georgios didn't believe in wallowing for long, and he'd picked himself up and dusted himself down. The next hour or two until their return had whirled by with the familiar routines of clearing the breakfast dishes, making the beds and wiping down the bathrooms. These daily chores in the high season carried him through the first few months of grief after Ana died because he couldn't allow standards to slip at Kyrgios's.

Now he and his Irish guests were about to drive to his old friend Konstantino's place. Wendy had come to wave them off once it had been decided the women and the little boy would venture down the old path to Oia by donkey while he would drop their men and the babies in Oia. Donal, the man who looked like the country music singer Kenny Rogers, had already had a quiet word to see if he could recommend somewhere they could while away the wait with a cold beer and plate of calamari overlooking the serenely still basin of water below. They would meet the women outside the resort where the son getting married was staying at ten to one, but if they didn't get going soon, they'd cut it too fine for the planned donkey ride.

He twisted in the driver's seat to see how everyone was getting on. 'Do you need some help?'

'No. We're grand, thanks, Georgios. That's it,' Aisling clicked her seatbelt, having finished securing Aoife in her baby carrier. 'Quinn?'

'All buckled.'

'We're all set,' Maureen fidgeted excitedly next to Donal.

'Okay then, let's go meet some donkeys!' Georgios gunned the engine and pulled away from the pension.

'Why are you afraid of donkeys, Quinn?' Moira asked as they sped down the road.

'I'm not. Who told you that? And I don't think you're in a position to comment given you're terrified of goats.'

'Aisling, of course, and a goat is a very different animal to a donkey. You can't compare apples to oranges. Besides you were there. You saw me nearly got inappropriately mauled by a Billy Goat.'

'True enough but I've no clue where Ash got that from because I don't have a problem with donkeys.'

'Your nose will grow Quinn Moran! You are so afraid of donkeys. You told me so yourself, although you'd not explain why.' Aisling defended herself.

'G'won then tell us, Quinn,' Roisin urged.

'He won't, Rosi, I've tried,' Aisling shook her head. 'To be honest, I'm worried about the chafing from the donkey riding. You don't know whether we'll be wearing those things cowboys slap about in, do you, Georgios?'

'Chaps.' Shay supplied.

'I don't think you will be needing the chaps.' Georgios struggled to keep a straight face.

'I think they've a very wise old face on them, the donkeys,' Maureen entered the discussion. 'You're not to be frightened of them, Quinn. They won't hurt you, will they, Georgios?'

Georgios glanced into the rear-view mirror, 'No, you will be quite safe. Donkeys are very affectionate and intelligent animals. Did you know they are considered the philosophers of the equine world?'

'No, I didn't know that. Did you know that girls?'

'No, Mammy,' the three sisters replied.

'That's very interesting, so. You see, Quinn, there's nothing to be frightened of.' Maureen reached over and patted his knee. 'And I don't know why we're even discussing you being frightened of them in the first place because it's not you going for the donkey ride now, is it?'

'I AM NOT FRIGHTENED OF FECKING DONKEYS.'

And so it went all the way to Konstantinos's Donkey Farm.

These Irish were a mad lot, Georgios grinned as he pulled up the hand brake. But they were good for the soul, too.

Chapter Nine

♥

'Yassas! Welcome. I am Konstantinos.' A craggy man whose face was evidence of a life lived outdoors greeted the group as they piled out of the van onto the dusty forecourt. They found themselves standing in front of a somewhat dilapidated building. Quinn stayed buckled in his seat, refusing to get out.

'I'll look after Aoife and Connor while you all have a look around. There's no point unsettling them for the sake of five or so minutes.' That was his story, and he was sticking to it.

'He's sulking,' Aisling mouthed at Roisin. 'And he is frightened of donkeys no matter what he says.'

'He's being an ass.' Moira giggled at her weak joke while her sisters groaned.

Maureen watched Georgios and Konstantinos slapping each other on the back heartily as though they were long-lost brothers. There was something about Konstantinos. He reminded her of someone. But who? Then it came to her. Of course! And she elbowed Donal, whispering out the corner of her mouth. 'Doesn't yer donkey man there put you in mind of Willie Nelson.'

'I was trying to work out who he reminded me of, and you're bang on Mo. Although I'd say he's a good few years younger than Willie,' Donal whispered back.

'And he doesn't have the plaits,' Bronagh added, overhearing.

'Or the bandana,' Roisin leaned over, keeping her voice low.

'Maybe if he had a guitar,' Leonard said to Bronagh.

'Personally, I'd see the resemblance if he'd a cowboy hat on,' this from Aisling also earwigging.

'He's nothing like yer Willie Nelson wan.' Moira finished getting the last word in because Georgios had begun a round of introductions involving hearty handshakes and more backslapping.

'Yassas!' Konstantinos repeated once the menfolk had had a good thwack, children being the only exception. He shook the women's hands and held onto Maureen's for a beat too long.

'You have good strong teeth for a woman of your years.'

'Erm, thank you.' Maureen was flustered by the unusual compliment, but she was also a woman never to miss an opportunity. 'You see, girls, the flossing in the evening pays off.'

'You would like a look around my farm, nai?'

'Grand,' was the collective murmuring, and Kiera, attached to her daddy's hip, gave an affirmative shout of 'Me!'

Konstantinos might be a few years younger than Willie, but he was older than Georgios and was dressed simply in an old check shirt and battered jeans with dusty leather boots despite the day's warmth. His grey hair was scraggly, and his beard matched while the yellow gnashers he revealed beaming at Kiera could rival any ass.

Kiera instantly took to him, giggling her head off at the sight of his full-wattage grin. 'Aga,' she demanded using her word for 'again' as she clapped her hands, but their Greek guide was already gesturing for them to follow him through the building they'd parked in front of.

'Leonard, you'd look very well in the blue jeans and boots like yer man there.' Bronagh said.

Leonard, who'd opted for walk shorts, socks and Roman sandals, wasn't convinced.

It was getting hot, Maureen thought, reminding herself to make sure Aisling put another layer of sunscreen on before they set off on the donkey ride. She'd be like a tomato before the day was out otherwise. The brief respite from the intense sun was welcome as they passed through the shade of what served as Konstantinos's office. There were sheaves of paper scattered over the desk and ungainly computer chords posing a health and safety hazard. Maureen wondered what a donkey farmer did precisely, other than the obvious. All too soon, though, they were blinking in the sunshine again, waiting for their eyes to readjust to the bright light.

The area out the back of the building was arid in the aftermath of summer. It was punctuated by a solitary hardy fig tree along with a smattering of olive trees which offered patchy shade to the donkeys housed inside the sizeable wire-fenced enclosure in front of them. The animals not clustered under the trees were mooching about the stony ground. Maureen would have felt sad for them if not for the mangers filled with plenty of straw for them to munch on and water troughs full to the brim. She saw they'd shelter, too, noting the stable building on the right-hand side of the pen. A mound of dried droppings was piled into a wheelbarrow near the fence line. Just outside the gate to the enclosure, six of the animals, compatriots, were tethered and already saddled up as they awaited their charges.

'I love the smell of farms.' Maureen inhaled the unmistakable earthy odour of animals. 'Being a country girl and all.'

'She'll be getting about in her wellies, wearing a head scarf and brown mac, driving a Land Rover, if you're not careful, Donal, what with her being a country girl and all,' Moira said.

'I think you just described the Queen,' Aisling replied.

Moira didn't reply, however. Instead, she was transfixed by Kiera's expression as Tom carried her over to the smallest of the tethered donkeys. 'Ah, look at her wee face, Mammy.'

Wonder and delight were evident in how Kiera's pudgy hands reached toward the little animal.

Maureen's smile watching her granddaughter, was indulgent.

Tom asked Konstantinos if it would be alright if he sat Kiera on the donkey she was trying to grab hold of for a photograph.

'Of course.' Konstantinos flashed those teeth again, but this time there were no giggles from Kiera because she was too intent on the donkey. 'But these animals here are mules, not donkeys, and they're very strong. This makes them good for carrying the heavy load.'

'Charming,' Bronagh mumbled.

'What's the difference between a donkey and a mule?' Shay asked, scratching one of the docile animals behind its ear. The trinity knot tattoo on his shoulder was visible beneath the singlet top he'd opted to wear. Upon seeing it for the first time at breakfast earlier, Maureen, forgetting she and Shay weren't making eye contact, had remarked that at least it wasn't the name of his ex-girlfriend like that fella Moira had stepped out with. 'What sort of a gombeen gets a name like Muireanne inked on himself?' she'd stated more than asked while Tom wanted to know, and not for the first time, exactly how many boyfriends Moira had had before he happened along. Roisin burning her toast had been a mercy which had moved the conversation away from Moira's exes and onto the perils of eating things that had been burned.

'Ah, I am glad you asked,' Konstantinos said, tugging at an ex-tra-long bit of his beard. 'A mule has a donkey father and a horse mother.'

Why he was glad they'd asked remained unclear as he veered away from the unfussy mating habits of equine animals to tell them a little about how integral to Santorini mules were. Without them, nothing could have been built on the Caldera. Not only that, but in the days before the chairlift and proper roading, a mule or donkey ride to the village above the harbour was the only option other than travelling by foot for visitors.

'Well, I'm after learning all sorts, aren't you, Bronagh? I mean, who'd have thought it, a donkey and a horse, like,' said Maureen.

Bronagh hadn't moved past that first piece of interbreeding trivia, and she nodded her agreement.

'I tell you something else few people know about the donkey.' Kon-stantinos leaned toward Bronagh and Maureen. Both women took a wary step back. Maureen hoped it was only horses and the like the donkeys were keen on because she wasn't sure how she'd feel about them if they were tarred with the same brush as those neighbours of hers, Amanda and Terence, who were into the swinging. 'Their coats,' Konstantinos tugged at his sleeve, 'they're not protecting them from the rain like a horse's coat would, so they need shelter, or they can get sick.'

'They'd need a bloody great big barn in Ireland then,' Moira piped up, digging her camera out. 'Gentle Kiera, don't go pulling the poor mule's ears now,' she warned as she pointed the camera at her. 'Tom smile, you eejit.' She lowered the camera. 'Actually, Leonard, would you do the honours?' Moira didn't wait for an answer, passing her camera to Bronagh's beau so she could join Tom and Kiera in the picture.

Not wanting to miss out on her granddaughter's first mule encounter, Maureen took action and retrieved her camera. 'Moira, would you lift your chin like so, and Tom, if you could turn your head a little to the left.'

'Mammy, get on with it, would you,' Moira sniped, pulling a face just as Maureen clicked. The photo op ended abruptly when the mule decided to do its business, and Tom hastily lifted Kiera off.

'Well, you ruined that one, didn't you, Moira, with a face on you like you'd just trod in the mule manure there?' Maureen put her camera away. 'All I wanted was a nice, normal family photograph for the album.'

'They're huge poos, Mummy,' Noah said to Roisin, staring at the steaming pile in fascination. He had a stick in his hand he'd found somewhere between the van and where they were now standing. It was twitching.

'Don't even think about it,' Roisin growled as her son stepped toward the mound stick, quivering like a beachcomber's metal detector.

'If the ladies are to reach Oia in time for their luncheon, then I think you best be on your way,' Georgios said to Konstantinos, who nodded and began untying the mule Kiera had just been bouncing on. 'I think Nico here will be perfect for young Noah.'

'Thank you,' Roisin mouthed as her son dropped the stick and forgot about the poo on the ground by Nico's business end in his excitement at being picked up and placed on top of the placid animal.

'Look at me, Nana, Poppa D!' Noah urged. 'His name's Nico. We've got lots in common, like our names have four letters and begin with 'N'.'

'That's grand, so it is, Noah. You've a tight hold of those reins there now, haven't you?' Maureen queried.

'We'll definitely be in Oia before one o'clock, Konstantinos, because the twins there will need feeding then?' Aisling double-checked.

'I can assure you we will be there in time.'

'I'll see you soon, Kiera.' Moira planted a kiss on top of her daughter's head, but Kiera, catching sight of Noah sitting on her mule, reins in hand, ready for the off, was not happy. Her face crumpled.

'Mine! Me! Mine!'

'We'll be off then,' Tom said hastily as Kiera began to sob like a river bursting its banks. He hurried back the way they'd come, throwing a 'Grand meeting you Konstantinos. I'll see you in Oia girls, enjoy yourselves now,' over his shoulder as he carted a squalling Kiera away. Georgios made plans to see his friend again soon, and there was much slapping of the back while Donal blew Maureen a kiss which she pretended to catch. Aisling and Moira made gagging faces, and Roisin would have too, but she was busy snogging the face off Shay. Leonard made to peck Bronagh on the cheek, but she turned so his puckered lips landed on her own and, grabbing hold of him, gave him a lingering kiss goodbye.

'If it's good enough for the young ones there, it's good enough for us,' she said, patting his red-faced cheek once she'd released him.

Meanwhile, Aisling had prised her sister and Shay apart. 'It's only a mule ride she's after going on Shay. She's not trekking the Great Divide or the like. On yer bike now.'

The three men trooped off with Georgios while Moira, her head tilted to one side and a frown firmly embedded between her brows, said, 'I think Kiera's going to take it to the next level, Mammy. I know that pitch, and it's not good. Tom will have a sod of a job trying to buckle her in her car seat. So I think you and Donal will have to break out the big guns and sing the song if they're to make it to Oia.'

Maureen cocked her ear, too, listening out. 'You're right, Moira,' she said before turning to Konstantinos, who was checking the saddle of the white mule. 'Would you excuse me just a moment? 'Tis only myself and her Poppa D can settle the toddler Kiera when she's in a state like so. She's a fan of country music, and when we sing her favourite song, 'Islands in the Stream', we're like the toddler whisperers, so we are. I do the Dolly part, of course.'

The weathered Santorini local hid his bafflement by dipping his head to signal she was excused.

'Thanks a million. I'll be as quick as I can, like. You sort the others out, but I'd like to ride the nice chestnutty-brown one over there. Thanks a million.' Maureen pointed to the animal she was referring to before hurrying off.

'I wanted to ride the brown one,' Aisling said to no one in particular.

Tom, who, as Moira predicted, was wrestling with their child, caught sight of Maureen hurrying over and straightened, smacking his head on the van's roof. Maureen couldn't hear what he said over the top of the cries but thought this was probably just as well as he thrust Kiera at her nana gratefully.

Donal didn't need to be asked. He knew the drill and was already clambering down from the van. He stood next to Maureen. 'Count of three, Mo.'

'Count of three, Donal.'

Georgios, who'd forgotten how loud a small child's protesting cries were, watched in amazement as the big Irish man opened his mouth.

'A one, a two, a one, two, three, four,' Donal launched into song.

That was the count of four, not three, Georgios thought, his eyes widening further when Maureen stepped into warble lyrics he knew well. 'Islands in the Stream', it was a favourite of his.

'Donal there fronts a Kenny Rogers tribute band, and Maureen duets with him on a few songs, like this one. Kiera loves it,' Tom explained, clocking Georgios's expression. 'Her nana and Poppa D singing 'Islands in the Stream' to her is the only thing that settles her when she gets herself worked up. Watch.'

It was true, Georgios thought as the little girl's face slowly relaxed, and her cries became hiccups. Finally, she fixed her watery eyes on her nana and then her poppa, and they shone with unadulterated adoration. When the song drew to a close, she was putty in their hands and allowed herself to be strapped into her seat.

'A miracle,' Georgios declared, knowing he'd not have believed what had just happened had he not witnessed it with his own eyes. Then, not wasting any more time, he pulled the van door shut and hopped behind the wheel, hoping the engine noise would have as much of a soothing effect on the little girl as the country music song had.

Maureen waved them off, coughing in the cloud of exhaust fumes as they exited the parking lot. Then she turned around, saying out loud, 'C'mon now, Maureen O'Mara, you've a date with a mule, so you have.'

Chapter Ten

♥

'It's just as well we're in fine fettle for our age, Bronagh.' Maureen looked behind her to where Bronagh sat proud and erect upon a black mule called Maxime.

'You are a fine Molly, as you English say.' Konstantinos treated Maureen to a wink.

'What's a Molly?' Maureen asked.

'A woman mule.'

Maureen was unsure whether to take being called a female mule, even a fine one, as a compliment, so she ignored the comment and continued to address Bronagh. 'You've got the posture of a woman half your age, so you have.' She gave Athena, the chestnut mule she'd bagsed, a quick pat and slotted her foot into the dangling stirrup. 'It's like riding a bike. It will all come back to me,' she said with concentration etched on her face as she attempted to haul herself up.

'I don't remember you ever telling us you had a donkey when you were a girl, mammy.'

'Athena here is a mule, Roisin. Are your ears painted on? And I didn't have a donkey or a mule, but I did have a donkey ride along the New Brighton beach in Liverpool once.' Then, finally, she swung her leg over the saddle on her third attempt. Once she was astride Athena with the reins in her hands, and she'd stopped panting, she addressed Bronagh once more. 'I know of a few women from the line dancing group who'd be unable to cock a leg over like so.'

'Sure, you look like you were born to the mule riding perched up there like so, Maureen,' Bronagh replied. 'You're a natural, so you are.'

'It's a shame the same can't be said of herself over there,' Maureen inclined her head toward Aisling, struggling to mount her steed.

'That's not helpful, Mammy, and I don't know whose stupid idea this was in the first place.' Aisling was getting red in the face because she couldn't get the momentum needed to hoist herself over and onto her allocated mule.

'Sure, it's like the gymnastics when you were told you needed more bounce, Aisling.'

'I hated gymnastics, as you well know, and the cross country, hockey, tennis, the lot of it,' Aisling muttered. 'And don't start going on about the romper shorts, sore tummies and the soldier on song.'

'I will help you.' Konstantinos placed his hands on Aisling's hips, making her jump.

'Houston, we have lift off,' Moira intoned, seeing Aisling's fright at the little Greek man's placement of his hands get her airborne. She landed atop Penelope, a fawn mule who wasn't phased by the sudden landing.

'Aisling, did you put plenty of sunscreen on? You don't want to be a tomato when we reach Oia.' Maureen remembered her earlier note to self as she eyed her middle child's lily-white arms.

'I did, Mammy.' Aisling kept hold of the reins with one hand and pulled her hat down low with the other.

Roisin and Moira nimbly alighted the two animals named Cora and Apollo while Konstantinos untied his chosen ride, Zeus. He addressed his group of riders who were raring to get going now they all had hold of the reins in a commanding tone. 'Listen to what I say, and we will have an enjoyable and relaxing trek to Oia.'

'We're listening, aren't we, girls?' Maureen looked from one to the other.

'We are.'

'And me, Nana.'

'And Noah's listening to Konstantinos.'

'Okay, so, mules, despite what many people think, they are not stubborn. They're merely careful and will never put themselves in danger. So if you are trying to get them to do something and they feel it is unsafe for them to do so, they will not move. In this respect, they are more intelligent than you and I. They are also sure of the foot.'

'He means surefooted,' Maureen whispered in case anyone hadn't caught the gist of what Konstantinos was telling them.

'You can put your trust in them,' he elaborated.

Just then, there was the unmistakable sound of someone/something breaking wind.

'It was Apollo,' Moira insisted, cheeks flaming as fingers pointed her way.

Konstantinos ran through a few basic instructions about guiding their mules which involved holding on and following the mule in front. Then, he informed them they'd be joining the ancient path to Oia at just over a mid-way point from where it began. He set off with a gentle clicking, giddy-up sort of noise. The remaining mules dutifully filed off one by one. Bronagh was behind Konstantinos, followed by Maureen, Moira, Aisling, Noah and Roisin. As they trotted along, a few nervous giggles sounded as the six inexperienced riders got used to the motion. Although Maureen would beg to differ on the inexperienced front as she stated confidently, 'Oh yes, it's all coming back to me now.'

'You're not Celine Dion, Mam.' Roisin called from the back.

'I'm going to have 'It's All Coming Back to Me Now' stuck in my head for the duration of this ride, thanks very much, Rosi,' Aisling grumbled.

'Fecky-show-off,' Moira said under her breath. 'One donkey ride half a century ago, and she thinks she's Frankie Dettori.'

By the time they'd plodded away from the farm, having picked their way across stony paddocks to the path carved into the dry earth, the initial white-knuckled grips on the reins had loosened. Their mule train had settled into a rhythmic clopping, and the autumn song of the hardiest cicadas was only broken by Apollo's letting off.

'Christ on a bike, Apollo, there's putting me in mind of Nanna Dee! Remember how you took your life in your hands if you walked up the stairs at O'Mara's behind her?' Roisin exclaimed.

The sisters giggled at the memory, and Maureen joined in remembering the old harridan's windy problem well.

'I apologise for Apollo,' Konstantinos called back over his shoulder. 'He has always been the same. His digestion, it is not good.'

'Thanks a million for giving me the farty mule,' Moira said in a voice not designed to carry.

'I don't know what you're moaning about,' Aisling griped. 'It's not you riding along in the line of fire.' She shifted, trying to get comfortable. 'These saddles are very hard. I'm definitely in for some chafing.'

'I'd have thought you'd have had plenty of padding there, Ash,' Moira threw back.

'Sic her, Penelope,' Aisling urged, but Penelope showed no interest in nipping at the woman sitting on Apollo.

The landscape was almost lunar-like until they rounded a bend, and there was a collective, gasp. It was their first glimpse of the famous

Caldera, and for a moment, they were rendered silent by the contrast between the dramatic red and black volcanic hills plunging into the deep blue water. It was striking.

'Now I know what Donal's been making such a fuss about. Did you ever see such a sight in your life?' Maureen said, her mouth hanging open.

It would have been unanimous that none of them ever had, but Noah was too busy telling Nico all about Mr Nibbles and Stef to comment.

'Will we get the chance to stop and take some photographs, Konstantinos?' Roisin called up the line.

'We will stop at Stavros. See the church up ahead there?'

Roisin followed the line of his finger to where a white speck was slotted into the hillside in the distance. 'Yes.'

'It is very old and traditional, and you can take good photos there. We will stop for a fifteen-minute break.'

'Did you hear that, Mammy?' Moira queried. 'So, don't be getting any ideas about letting go of the reins to fetch your camera.'

'I know what I'm doing, Moira.'

The combination of awe-inspiring views, warmth from the midday sun, and insect song mingling with the hypnotically slow thud of the mules' hooves and Noah's gerbil monologue was having an almost sedative-like effect on the group. So it was when Maureen spoke up, her voice carried on the gentle breeze that had begun blowing now they were in the open above the Caldera, causing them all to startle and readjust themselves in the saddle.

'Do you know it's come to me now that this is how the Blessed Mother Mary herself must have felt riding the donkey to Bethlehem with Joseph there leading the way?'

'Maureen, this is nothing like Mary and Joseph because Mary was about to give birth,' Bronagh remarked. She patted her middle. 'Bloating is not the same thing.'

'Mammy, you can't compare yourself to Mary there. There was nothing immaculate about Patrick's conception. He looks far too much like Daddy for that,' Aisling said.

'I'm not after comparing myself. I'm just saying, like. And I remember full well the night your brother was conceived because the heating was off. Can you imagine? In a place the size of O'Mara's. There was nothing else for it but to have an early night.'

'And for another thing, Maureen, the Blessed Mother Mary was riding side-saddle,' Bronagh added. 'I wouldn't fancy that myself. I'm more Boudicca than the Virgin Mary, me.'

'No wonder the babby Jesus was desperate to be born with all the jostling about like,' Moira added thoughtfully. 'It's a wonder they made it to the stable at all. Maybe they should put the mammies-to-be who run late with their babbies on a mule for half an hour. It would kick things off.'

'I can just see them now doing circuits of the Holles Street Hospital, car park by mule,' Roisin remarked.

'I wonder if Mary was after chafing,' Aisling pondered further.

'No, she wasn't Aisling because she was riding side-saddle,' Bronagh repeated herself.

'I wonder if I should try that?'

'Don't even think about it Aisling. You'll be rolling off down into the Caldera there before you know it, and I won't be coming in after you,' Moira said.

Maureen's voice overrode them all, 'But the Blessed Mother Mary riding on the donkey to Bethlehem has got me thinking,' Maureen continued.

'Ah no, Mammy, not the thinking,' Moira said.

'What if Luke got it wrong in the gospel and the donkey was a mule?'

Maureen's profound sentence rendered them silent for a split second until Moira spoke up, 'Jaysus wept, Mammy! It's only the fifth mystery of the Rosary you're after finding the answer to. We know all about praying for the five parts of the Joyful, Sorrowful, Glorious and Luminous Mysteries, but now we've got a fifth to add to the Rosary, The Donkey Mysteries.'

'Or the Mule Mysteries,' Aisling sniggered.

Roisin made them all snort by adding, 'Or the Ass Mysteries.'

'I'd give you all a thick ear if you were closer,' Maureen shot back at her daughters. 'Close your ears there, Noah.'

The conversation was all over the top of the little boy's head because Apollo's constant farting was entertaining him thoroughly.

'You're not to be making fun of the sacred mysteries.' Maureen crossed herself, and at the exact moment as she dropped the reins with her right hand, Bronagh's mule, Maxime, decided to make a lunge for Maureen's Athena, nipping her on the backside. The chestnut mule brayed her indignance and performed a 180-degree turn with Maureen's right arm swinging in the air as she clung to the reins with her left hand like she was in the Rodeo. Instead of shouting, 'Yeehaw!' she shrieked, 'Holy God Above Tonight!'

'Whoa there, Maxime, whoa.' Bronagh was being jigged about as she tried to get her feisty boy under control.

'Mammy, hold on!' Moira and the others urged, and their eyes bulged in horror as Athena reared back on her hind legs.

'I can't!' were Maureen's last words.

Chapter Eleven

'Mammy, are you alright?' all three sisters cried out as Maureen toppled off the back of Athena and onto the hard ground.

'Oof!' The air was knocked out of her, and she sat there dazed while Konstantinos wasted no time in dismounting, firing off a few rapid words in Greek that saw both the animals stop baring their teeth at one another and settle just as the toddler Kiera did to the 'Islands in the Stream' song.

'The ass whisperer,' Moira breathed as Maxime began snuffling at the ground the picture of innocence while Athena turned herself around and gently nosed Maureen as if to say, 'What on earth are you doing down there?'

'Maureen,' Konstantinos held his hand out, and Maureen grasped it, allowing him to help her to her feet.

Upon seeing she was upright, Bronagh shooed away the group of hikers who were decked out like they meant business. They'd paused with morbid fascination to watch the unfolding mule massacre. 'The show's over,' she called out, giving an extra flap of her hand.

As for Maureen, she didn't want them fretting, so she raised the hand Konstantinos had hold of victoriously, crying out, 'I'm alive!' Then, letting go of their overly friendly guide's grasp, she tried a lunge on both legs to prove her point before rotating her head to the left and right and giving her shoulders a roll for good measure.

'Nothing's broken then, Mammy?'

'No thanks to you three.' Maureen glowered at her offspring.

Konstantinos made to brush the dusty dirt off her backside, and when Maureen gave him short shrift, the hikers hesitated, not wishing to miss any further drama, but Konstantinos held both his hands up in the international sign of surrender, and so they continued their hillside climb.

'Mammy, you had us worried when you rolled off the back of Athena like so,' Aisling said. 'It was like watching an action scene in a film unfold in slow motion.'

'Sure, keeping me down would take more than a wee tumble. I've got a sore backside, and I've no doubt there'll be a bruise or two by the morning, but it's nothing the E45 cream won't fix. Anyway, it's a bit late to say you were worried now. Given it's down to you, you and you,' she jabbed a finger at Moira, Aisling and Roisin, 'I fell off Athena here in the first place.'

'How do you figure that?' Roisin screwed her face up, bewildered as to the correlation between events.

'It's your blasphemous mouths that are to blame for my near-death experience there.'

It wasn't quite a clap of thunder, but all hell had let loose after joking about the sacred Mysteries of the Rosary, and the sisters looked at each other, not wanting anything else to befall their group between here and Oia. *There was nothing else for it*, they silently communicated with each other. *They'd have to apologise*.

'Sorry, Mammy, I was only joking.' Roisin, as the oldest sister, went first.

'And me,' Aisling added.

'Me too, Mammy,' Moira finished.

'It's not me you should be saying you're sorry to now, is it?' Maureen raised her eyes heavenward, giving them a hefty hint as to whom she had in mind.

The three sisters tilted their chins skyward and murmured a sorry.

The apologising wasn't over yet, though. Konstantinos went next. The Greek man placed his hand on his heart and, mournfully, said, 'I'm very sorry for what happened, everyone, especially for you, Maureen. But you must understand Maxime here is a man.' He nodded his head in the direction of the feisty mule. 'He's no longer a young man, but he still has needs, and there's Athena in the prime of her life, a mule with good strong teeth and years of experience prancing about waving her—'

'We get the idea thank you, Konstantinos.' Maureen interjected, giving herself one final dust down.

'Is he talking about the mule, there or Mammy?' Moira whispered, raising her eyebrows at her sisters.

They grinned at each other.

Bronagh was busy digging deep in her rucksack, and she pulled out a packet of custard creams, offering it to Maureen. 'A peace offering even though it wasn't technically my fault Maxime here attacked Athena. But I am guilty by association.'

Maureen helped herself, figuring the sugar hit would be good for the shock. A biscuit was the next best thing to a cup of tea, and there wasn't much chance of one of those.

'You didn't tell us you had those,' Moira said accusingly.

'A girl's got to have some secrets now,' Bronagh said, and once Maureen had taken the biscuit, she offered one to Konstantinos before taking one herself and passing them down the line.

'And you know I need regular snacks, Bronagh,' Aisling added. 'So I'll be taking two.'

'And I'm a growing boy, so I'll take three.' Noah said.

'Bronagh,' Maureen said once she'd finished munching, 'if you don't mind, it would be best if you and Maxime rode behind Konstantinos.' She hoisted herself back on the placidly waiting Athena and gingerly arranged herself on the saddle.

'Of course.' Bronagh duly nudged Maxime around Maureen and Athena, who were ignoring one another now, to slot in behind Zeus.

'We are only a few minutes from the church. We shall stop and take a photograph there,' Konstantinos said before mounting Zeus and geeing them on their way.

***

The lonely, white church with its bell presiding over the hill and Caldera was, just as Konstantinos had promised a worthy photo stop. He was put in charge of doing the rounds with the cameras as they posed on their mules, wanting to preserve the setting on film forever. Then, they slid off, eager to give their saddle-sore bottoms a break and explore the interior of the church.

It was simple inside but refreshingly cool, and if they'd thought their journey couldn't get any more achingly sublime, then the sight of Oia cascading like the white foam on a wave over the cliff edge ahead proved them wrong.

'It makes sense to me now,' Maureen murmured in a quiet voice, only Bronagh caught.

'What's that then, Maureen?' Bronagh asked, half twisting her head to hear her friend's reply.

'I can see why Cindy and Pat wanted to marry here. This place must be heaven on earth.'

'I think you're right, Maureen, and we've not even seen the sunset yet. That's what Oia's famous for.'

Maureen wasn't listening, though, because as she continued to soak in the vista growing ever close, she was, for once, lost for words.

Chapter Twelve

♥

'Goodbye, Konstantinos,' Maureen called out, with the rest of the easy riders' voices joining hers in waving the little mule man off. He'd delivered them on time to Oia relatively safely, a bruised bottom and general chafing aside. The cobbled lanes they'd ventured down to reach their destination had been crowded, with Konstantinos explaining several cruise ships had docked. It explained the hordes of sightseers pondering the pottery, jewellery, sarongs and paintings all competing for their attention. The day-trippers had to flatten themselves against pale salmon and blue walls to let their convoy pass or risk being trampled, and Maureen felt very important sitting up high like so as the crowds parted to allow the mule caravan through.

The resort where Patrick, Cindy, and her family were staying was tucked away on the left of the lane they'd come to a halt on. It was hidden behind a large timber door and offered no hint as to what might lie behind it. The only clue they'd the right place was the discreet Azure Waters nameplate next to the door. When they said their goodbyes to Maxime, Athena, Penelope, Apollo, Cora and Nico, then to Zeus and Konstantinos, the time was precisely 12.45 pm as per Maureen's decree. She thought it was better to be early than late and was excited about seeing her son. It had been too long between visits. She was also anxious about what sort of a family her firstborn would marry into. Where were Donal and the others? she thought, checking her watch.

'He's like the Pied Piper of Santorini, only with mules and not rats. Look at them following Konstantinos like so,' Roisin said as her ride, Cora, disappeared.

'Don't be mentioning rats now, Roisin. Look, the hairs on my arms are standing on end just hearing the word.' Bronagh pulled the sleeve of her shirt up to prove her point. She then launched into a story about the time Mrs Flaherty had spotted a rat in the courtyard out the back of O'Mara's. It was the only time she'd encouraged their regular visitor Foxy Loxy to pay them a call.

'They'll be here any minute, Mammy,' Aisling said, noting her checking her watch. 'The twins are due a feed for one thing.'

Noah's eyes lit up. Since having seen cows being milked on a farm visit, his Aunt Aisling breastfeeding his twin cousins was a source of fascination.

However, as the minutes began to tick by, Aisling, too, began to fidget agitatedly. 'Where are they? My boobs are getting sore. Quinn knows the babbies will be needing me.'

'Mammy, you did say 12.45, didn't you?' Moira asked, hoping Tom had given Kiera her lunch or she'd be a terrible grump by the time they got here, and she didn't want Cindy's family bearing witness to a hungry Kiera because it wasn't pretty.

'I did. I said to the menfolk, 12.45 prompt. You heard me yourselves. I hope they've not got themselves lost because Donal's never late. He prides himself on being a punctual man, does Donal.'

'My Lennie's got a good sense of direction, Maureen, so don't be worrying about them being lost. We did the Greenan Maze in Wicklow there, and he led us out in no time.' Bronagh's brow furrowed. 'But you can set your watch by him, and it's not like him to run behind schedule, not like him at all.'

Moira and Roisin remained silent. Their fellas weren't the best timekeepers, but then they'd the others to keep them in line. They should have been here by now, given the importance of the luncheon.

Maureen's face was beginning to turn a mottled red as checking the slim gold band on her wrist for the umpteenth time, she saw there were now only two minutes until they were expected and still no sign of them. Patrick would not be happy if they were late, and more to the point, what sort of an impression would they make on Cindy's family straggling in whenever it suited them? They'd think them a right rag-tag bunch of ill-mannered, eejit Irish holidaymakers.

'Breathe, Mammy,' Roisin instructed, running through her yoga breathing repertoire. 'Inhale, one, two, three. Now exhale one, two, three, four.'

Maureen stopped mid-exhale, cocking her head to one side. 'What's that noise?'

'What noise?' Moira asked.

'Shush, listen,' Bronagh said, her index finger raised to her lips.

They all craned to catch whatever Maureen was on about over the general hubbub.

Maureen frowned. 'It sounds like a load of football hooligans singing.'

'It does,' Bronagh agreed. 'Or a group of lads on a stag do in Temple Bar on a Saturday night.'

'Don't yer hooligan wans usually chant things like 'Football's coming Home'?' Moira asked.

'Or 'We are the Champions'?' Aisling added.

'Isn't that 'Roll out the Barrel' they're after singing?' Roisin frowned.

'It is,' Maureen and Bronagh replied in unison.

The singing grew closer, and as the culprits rounded the same bend Konstantinos and the mules had not long disappeared around, everyone's mouth, including Noah's, fell open.

'I don't believe it.' Maureen was the first to speak with the others, having been rendered silent by the sight of Leonard, who appeared to be the ringleader of the motley crew waving his arm about like a conductor in Roman sandals as the lads behind him gave the Beer Barrel Polka their all.

'Lennie was a choirboy,' Bronagh offered up lamely.

'Be that as it may, Bronagh, there's nothing pure and angelic about that lot there,' Maureen snipped as her hands found a home firmly on her hips.

Bronagh marched down the cobbles, and the singing petered out as she hauled Leonard aside for a quiet word.

Donal, clocking Maureen, said something out the corner of his mouth to Quinn, Tom and Shay, and the four of them approached the hatchet-faced women, silently, doing their best to walk in a straight line.

'I think they've been drinking, Mammy,' Moira said with the sanctimonious tone of a teetotaller. 'They've all got that look on their faces.'

'Like little boys with their hands caught in the biscuit tin,' Maureen said. She had a feeling Moira was right.

'They're putting me in mind of Pat when you'd catch him pretending to look at his Whizzer and Chips Annual, but you could tell by the look on his face he'd a girlie magazine hidden in it,' Aisling said.

There was no time for further debate because the fellas were close enough now for Maureen to catch the whiff of ale coming off them. She leaned in close to Donal, who puckered up, hoping he might not be in the bad books after all and exclaimed, 'You've got the beery breath

Donal McCarthy, and we've only a minute to spare until we're due to meet Pat, Cindy and her family for lunch!'

'That's good because I'm starving, me. We shared a plate of calamari, but it was on the chewy side, and I only had the one-piece,' Quinn said, then wisely buttoned it as his wife glared at him, snatching hold of the baby carrier containing Aoife.

'My boobs are fit to burst here.'

'Sorry, Ash,' Quinn slurred. 'We only had a pint or two.'

'It was very hot, you see,' Shay said as Roisin took hold of Connor's carrier, giving him a death stare.

'We were only going to have the one.' Tom explained to Moira, who was trying to wipe Kiera's face. Judging by the red sauce around her mouth, she'd had something to eat at least.

'But then it seemed like a good idea to have another,' Shay explained.

'Two pints, my arse,' Moira muttered, stashing the wet wipe in the baby bag Tom was also carrying.

'Never mind all that now,' Maureen said. 'Who's got some peppermints? I'll not have you lot meeting the Berkeley's with the beery breath.'

Pockets were hastily patted down, and Moira produced a tube of gum which was quickly passed around the fellas, Leonard included.

'Chew!' Maureen ordered, and once she saw the menfolk's jaws going like the clappers, she moved to open Azure Waters door, but before doing so, she swung around and eyed first Leonard, then Donal, Shay, Tom and Quinn before fixing Leonard in her line of sight once more. 'Right, listen up. Before we step through that door, you promise me there'll be no more singing. The Berkleys do not want to be serenaded by 'Roll out the Barrel' while trying to enjoy their lunch. Understood?'

The menfolk stopped chewing long enough to give a loud, clear 'Understood.'

Chapter Thirteen

♥

Maureen opened the door to Azure Waters, and they stepped inside the resort's inner sanctum. Leonard, the last to enter, pulled the door closed and joined their group in the gleaming white foyer that seemed to be full of curving walls. The glass doors at the far end of the space were flung open to showcase an outdoor area for guests to enjoy the endless expanse of blue lapis lazuli. Despite the open doors, the aircon was set to cool, and there was an audible sigh of relief as it washed over them.

'Jaysus, Ita could learn a thing or two about making a place sparkle,' Bronagh said, glancing around, her dark eyes wide, soaking in the luxurious ambience.

'I might snap some photos to take home and show her,' Aisling said, agreeing with Bronagh as she fished her camera out to prove she was serious.

Maureen breathed in the heady scent of oriental lilies, and Roisin, a hay fever sufferer, began sneezing. She thought opulent was the word that sprang to mind, absorbing all the white, which would look cold and austere in Dublin. However, it was perfect, thanks to the glorious sunshine in Santorini. On her second sweep of the place, she found a few splashes of colour with the introduction of periwinkle shade in the furnishings, a canvas daubed in primary colours dominating one wall space. At the same time, the Azure Waters logo swirled behind the front desk in an azure statement. A modern fountain took centre stage, tinkling in a manner that would remind guests to go for one last wee before they ventured out for the day or, if they'd sunk into one of the sofas angled to enjoy the view outside, send them off to sleep.

The sound had a diuretic effect on Quinn, whom she overheard saying to his wife, 'That beer's going right through me. Can you see the jacks anywhere?'

'Tie a knot in it,' was Aisling's unsympathetic response as she clicked away with her camera.

A glance down at her capris and crumpled linen shirt made Maureen acutely aware of how sweaty and dusty she was. *Bronagh and the girls were no better*, she thought, checking them out with a sigh. It was too late to whip back to their pension for a quick shower and change of clothes, though. *Perhaps a mule ride before lunch hadn't been the brightest of ideas*, she mused, deciding there was nothing else for it; the Berkleys would have to take them as they found them.

'Jaysus wept. Pat must have money to burn,' Aisling said, shaking her head, the camera still in her hand. She'd momentarily forgotten about feeding the twins, what with all that glary white, cleanness and now the familiar rankle of her brother's easiness with other people's money, or more to the point, their mammy's, had flared.

'You girls have been looked after with your holidays and childcare,' Maureen replied through tight lips. Patrick and the ten thousand pounds he'd borrowed from her were a sore spot with her and her daughters. The difference being it annoyed her girls that Pat had the audacity to ask their mammy for money in the first place. It was money they said he'd no intention of paying back despite his smooth talk of interest on top of the loan repayment when he'd initially asked for help with a new venture.

Patrick was an entrepreneur, whatever that entailed, because even though Maureen had asked him to elaborate, his explanations as to what his business ventures were, were always vague. But he wasn't just a businessman. He was Maureen's only son who'd opted to go his way instead of following in his mammy and daddy's footsteps, and he'd needed a helping hand. What parent wouldn't help their child if they were able to? The niggly inner voice that queried whether Brian would have blithely handed over such a sum of money to a son who never seemed to stick at anything in particular was one she was quick to squash. However, Maureen wasn't a fool even if her girls thought her so where Pat was concerned. When agreeing to the loan, she'd known that was the last she'd see of that money. And, this was why, unbeknown to her daughters, the debt was being written off along with a Waterford crystal centrepiece bowl winging its way as a wedding present to the couple's address in Los Angeles. She'd tell Patrick this after the wedding.

Right now, though, was not the time to think of monies owed and gifts because a wedding was about new beginnings and happy ever afters. It was also about family and making the right impression on the Berkleys. Maureen wondered where they were staying and whether their accommodation was as luxurious as the happy couple's.

'This is gorgeous,' Moira breathed. 'Just think, Tom, one day when you're a qualified GP, and I'm a celebrated artist, we'll be able to stay at places like this.'

Tom shrugged, unimpressed. 'I quite like Kyrgios's Pension where we're staying. It's very comfortable beds aside, and from what I've gathered, the beds are like rocks all over the Greek Islands. This sort of accommodation always makes me feel I've to be on my best behaviour.'

'You've got to be on your best behaviour at Kyrgios's,' Maureen told Tom, and if she'd been fond of her future doctor-as-good-as-a-son-in-law before, she grew a little fonder hearing his sentiment because she agreed with him. Oh, there was no disputing Azure Waters was the epitome of elegant luxury, but it didn't have the welcoming warmth of Georgios's place. As the former proprietor of a guesthouse herself, she liked a place to feel like a home away from home.

The receptionist smiling at them wore her hair in a slicked-back bun. Her makeup was minimal, except for a dark red lip, and she was dressed in a crisp white shirt with the hotel's logo on the front pocket and a name badge with Petra Diakos displayed on it. The front desk she was standing to attention behind hid the rest of her uniform.

'Hello there.' Maureen approached the receptionist, peering at her name badge, 'Petra. We're here for the Berkeley family luncheon. It's my son Patrick O'Mara who's after getting married this week.'

'Of course. Welcome to Azure Waters. If you'd care to follow me.' Petra stepped around the desk, revealing a navy skirt and matching mules that tip-tapped across the tiled floor toward the glass doors.

'I've died and gone to heaven,' Moira stated as the party emerged onto the top veranda, greeted by white-iced, cake-like tiers descending to an infinity pool. A woman doing the breaststroke in a red swimsuit glided through the water while another couple admired the view at the water's edge, sipping exotic cocktails. Bronzed guests lazed on sun loungers on the bottom terraces or dined at the various tables set up here and on the veranda below. 'Look, there's Pat and Cindy!' she added.

Patrick had stood up from the long table shaded by two sun umbrellas where he, Cindy and her family were seated. Carafes of wine and little bowls of glistening olives littered the table. Maureen barely registered the rest of her son's guests as she charged down the stairs with her arms wide to greet him.

'Patrick!'

'Mammy!' Patrick had his arms ready to catch her as she flung herself at him. 'It's so good to see you.'

'It's like a scene from a film. You know where the son comes home from war,' Roisin said to Shay in a lowered voice. 'You watch. She'll pat him down next as customs do at the airport.'

Shay laughed as Maureen gave her son a quick pat down.

'Have you lost weight, Pat?' That Cindy wan always had him on some new fandangle diet or other. Mind, she should know better now she was eating for two. 'You need to eat more potatoes.'

'Cindy's been eating us out of house and home,' Patrick grinned, and Maureen blinked because his teeth were as blindingly white as their surroundings. It took her by surprise each time she saw him.

'Mom!'

Maureen, remembering why she was here in Santorini, reluctantly released her son and watched as Cindy struggled up from her seat. *Janey Mack, it was a good job Father Fitzpatrick wasn't here*, she thought. The poor priest would have a heart attack at the sight of Maureen's soon-to-be daughter-in-law looking like a ripe peach in a sprayed-on minidress as she waddled over to envelope her in a bosomy hug.

'Cindy, you're looking very erm well.' Maureen squeezed out between gasps for air.

Cindy giggled. 'I woke up one morning, Mom, and my belly had just ballooned, hadn't it, Pat?' she gushed in her little girl's voice.

'It had,' Patrick affirmed giving his fiancée a toothpaste advertisement smile between welcoming his family and honorary family with handshakes, hugs and kisses.

'Jaysus wept. He's looking more and more like Liberace with that smile each time we see him,' Aisling whispered in Moira's ear.

Moira hadn't a clue who she was referring to but she got the idea.

'You're getting plenty of rest and eating properly, I hope,' Maureen said.

'I am Mom. Patrick's been cooking up a storm each evening and ensuring I put my feet up. I had to cancel the Fresh as a Daisy Femfresh commercial because this wasn't the look they were wanting.' She patted her enormous tummy blissfully. 'But there's the possibility of an incontinence pad contract after our little O'Mara baby here's born.'

'Very good. Will you be taking Pat's name then?' Maureen asked hopefully.

'I will, Mom. I'm an old-fashioned kind of a gal.'

Not that old-fashioned you couldn't wait to get wed before you got yourself in the family way, Maureen thought, glancing down at Cindy's burgeoning middle, but Cindy was already moving on as, with a squeal of delight, she honed in on the rest of the Irish contingent.

'Hey there, my favourite nephew.'

Aisling bristled.

Cindy hastily reworded her greeting to, 'Hey there, my favourite, oldest nephew.'

Noah was swept up in pillowy, perfumy, peachy cuddle and had a daft expression when he removed himself from his Aunty Cindy's cleavage.

Maureen barely had time to mull over how she felt about the O'Mara family name being forever linked to incontinence pads before she was in danger of being impaled on the eyelashes of the woman embracing her. *So she must be Cindy's mammy, given how well-endowed she was*, Maureen thought, wondering if she'd ever be allowed up for air. At last, though, she was freed to find herself staring at a woman with the biggest hair she'd ever seen, hair and eyelashes for that matter.

'I'm Bea, Cindy's momma Mo-reen and ain't this just the berries? All of us here in the Greek Islands for our children's wedding. I do declare I'm just thrilled to meet y'all.' She laid a hand adorned with enormous sparkly rings and lethal weapon fingernails, in the same shade of coral as her lips, on her chest.

'Well, now it's very nice to meet you too,' Maureen offered by reply, wishing she had a repertoire of colourful sayings she could pull from her hat but didn't think *Holy God above tonight* or *Jesus, Mary and Joseph* fitted the bill. 'Bea, this is my live-in manfriend, Donal.'

'Doe-nell, it's a pleasure. Well, ain't you a fine figure of a man.' Bea grasped the startled Donal to her.

Maureen heard his muffled cry. 'It's Donal like a doughnut with all on the end.'

The embrace was too long for Maureen's liking, and it was a relief when Donal was freed, gasping like a guppy for air.

She'd barely finished smoothing Donal's hair when her hand was grasped, and her arm was in danger of becoming dislodged from its socket. The culprit was a bear of a man with a girth to rival his daughter's.

'Big Jim at your service Ma'am.'

'Maureen O'Mara.' Maureen absorbed the size of the man dressed like yer boss fella from that TV show Patrick had loved as a child with the orange car and the two lads always outwitting the law. She thought Big Jim's white suit and matching hat were very smart, giving him the once-over and thinking Donal should not have worn the flip-flops. At least his fungal toe infection had cleared up beautifully. That was something. Mind, she wasn't in a position to talk. Bea, who was being introduced to the rest of the family by Cindy and Patrick, was hardly slumming it in that floaty silk number. For the second time, Maureen thought a mule ride before lunch hadn't been a good idea. She should have been showcasing the wrap dress Ciara with a 'C', not a 'K', who worked at her favourite Howth clothing boutique, had said was perfect for a Greek holiday. Maureen had been hesitant initially because bold floral prints weren't her thing. They swamped her, but she trusted Ciara when she'd said she looked casual yet elegant and not like a sunflower with a head, as Moira had said. Ciara also pointed out busy prints were all the rage, and BO or burnt orange to those not in the know, was so last year. It was a shame because Maureen had thought that shade looked well on her. Fashion was fickle, she supposed.

'Join us.' Big Jim was hauling her over to the table now. 'I'm gonna sit you next to Sherry, Cindy's sister. Sherry, this here is Mo-reen.'

Maureen had her eye on Donal, who was being shepherded to a seat next to Bea, but not wanting to seem rude, she dragged her eyes away to greet the girl that could have been Cindy's twin.

'Hi there,' Sherry showed off her teeth. 'Can I call you Mom too? Cindy and I, we're real close. We share everything.' She tittered, 'But not Patrick, of course.'

Holy God Above Tonight. Maureen nodded. She was in shock, but the shocks weren't done yet.

Sweeping toward their table was another glamour puss only with iron-straight, red hair.

'Hello, hello, a thousand apologies. I was in the bathroom. I'm Bobby-Jean.' Bobby-Jean took the vacant seat next to Maureen. 'Now, let me guess. You must be Patrick's mom, Maureen. Am I right?'

Maureen, fixated on Bobby-Jean's enormous Adam's apple, nodded.

'It's a pleasure to meet you finally. Cindy's told me so much about you and your family.'

Bobby-Jean's voice was like loose gravel, Maureen thought, plastering a smile on her face as her brain scrambled to place this person because the name Bobby-Jean was one she knew she'd heard. *Bobby-Jean, Bobby-Jean*, she parroted to herself. Her jaw was in danger of hitting the flag-stoned veranda as she twigged. So this was who was going to be officiating over the wedding. What would Father Fitzpatrick have to say if he caught wind? She swooned at the thought of Rosemary Farrell's face when she showed her the wedding photos.

Chapter Fourteen

'Fetch her a glass of water, someone,' Donal urged, sitting Maureen down. The sight of his beloved Mo in a state of near collapse had sobered him as quickly as if someone had tossed a bucket of ice over him. 'I think she's had too much sun today. That's it, Mo, sit there.'

'Do the pranayama breathing, Mammy, as I showed you,' Roisin muscled in.

Maureen flopped gratefully down on the seat, feeling like she were the Southern belle, not Bea, Sherry and Cindy.

Aisling, having snatched up the water jug on the table, poured a tall glass and thrust it at her, 'Here, Mammy drink this. It might be the sunstroke you're after catching. Although you did have a hat on when we were out today.'

Not wanting to be left out, Moira flapped her hand in front of Maureen's face, 'Earth to Mammy, is anybody in there?'

Maureen wished they'd all disappear. Just for a moment, mind, so as she could reset herself. Her toes dug into the soles of her sandals. *Sure, the world would be boring if we were all the same*, she told herself, *and she was an open-minded woman who'd had a shock that was all.*

'Maybe it's the fall you had earlier,' Roisin wondered out loud. 'I don't think you hit your head, though.'

'What fall?' Donal's face creased in concern. 'Nobody mentioned a fall.'

'She fell off the back of Athena, the mule she was riding.' Roisin elaborated.

'How did you manage that?' Tom asked, joining the conversation. He looked genuinely interested.

'Bronagh's mule Maxime bit Athena, the mule Mammy was on. Anyway, Athena bucked, and you can hardly blame her. I would, too, if some eejit came along and bit me on the arse. Mammy didn't stand a chance,' Moira explained.

'At least Maxime didn't bite Mammy on the arse,' Aisling said.

All the female mule riders grimaced at the thought of the animal's big teeth coming after them.

Moira snickered, 'Or, Konstantinos.'

Roisin and Aisling grinned, and Roisin made noises about eating apples through tennis rackets.

Donal's eyes flicked between the sisters trying to make sense of what they were on about before shrugging his shoulders.

Noah, who'd been very quiet up to this point, pushed his way through to the fore. 'She's got a very sore bottom, haven't you, Nana?'

'She's got a name Noah, and I do.' Maureen spoke up at last. Then she raised her chin to meet the gaze of the concerned faces huddled around her, embarrassed by the fuss she'd caused in front of Cindy's family. 'It's alright. Sure, I'm grand now. I think Donal was right. It was too much sun is all,' she fibbed, swivelling around in her seat and picking up a menu to fan herself. She studiously avoided Bobby-Jean's eye.

'Well, I think we should all sit ourselves down and stop crowding Mo-reen here,' Big Jim rumbled, and he was so big that nobody dared argue as they all hastily bagsed a seat.

Bea rested her hand on Donal's forearm in a friendly manner that completely took Maureen's mind off what Father Fitzpatrick would say about Bobby-Jean.

Noah, sitting opposite Bobby-Jean, had his chin cupped in his hands and his elbows on the table as he stared in the way children do when they've something on their mind.

'Elbows off the table,' Roisin told her son.

Maureen watched as Noah did as he was told, but as he pressed his lips together and frowned, his focus still very much on the colourful wedding celebrant she was seated next to, her head began to throb. Maureen's fingertips began massaging her temples because she knew that look and had a fair idea of what her grandson was about to come out with. But, worst of all, there was nothing she could do about it without causing a scene either.

'Bobby-Jean, I'm Noah, and my mummy is Uncle Patrick's sister. The baby over there trying to grab the bread roll is my cousin Kiera and the two small ones that don't do anything are also my cousins. Are you Cindy's cousin because you don't look much like her?' Indulgent and slightly embarrassed smiles at his curiosity were directed his way while Maureen's toes curled to the point of cramping.

'No,' Bobby-Jean said equally earnestly. 'Cindy and I aren't related young man, but we are old friends. We used to share a house when she first moved to LA. 'We had so much fun. We're like sisters.'

'We sure did,' Cindy giggled across the table. 'Although I'm still unsure if you're forgiven for stretching my favourite LBD.'

'Little black dress,' Roisin supplied for Noah.

'And, I, among many other things, stylist to the stars, makeup artist, am also a celebrant.'

'Bobby-Jean's in high demand. We're so grateful you squeezed us in, aren't we, Pat? And,' her squeal was on a par with Kiera's, 'that you've agreed to do my wedding makeup.'

Patrick looked somewhat on the fence about the deal.

'It's my pleasure. And, you know I wouldn't miss being part of my best girl's big day for the world.' Bobby-Jean blew a kiss to Cindy.

'I don't understand. What's a celebrant?' Noah was still in the dark.

'A celebrant, my little friend, is a person who can marry people.'

'Like a priest?'

'Like a priest,' Bobby-Jean confirmed. 'Only I don't have to wear long white robes and give Mass.'

Heaven forbid, Maureen thought.

'So you get to do all the fun stuff?'

'You've got it.'

Noah digested this. Menus were snapped open, and Maureen began to relax. *No offence had been caused*, she thought, scanning the luncheon offerings. 'Hmm, moussaka sounds nice, Donal. What are you thinking?' She was pleased to see Bea's hand had removed itself from her manfriend's forearm as she held her menu in front of her.

'You hit the nail on the head with moussaka, Mo. That'll go down a treat.'

They smiled at one another, pleased that they were on the same page as usual, but then Maureen inhaled beery, minty breath closing the expanse between them and added primly, 'It will soak up all that beer.'

'Tom's going to need at least three of those bread rolls in the basket there, a starter, main and dessert if that's the case,' Moira said.

'So's Quinn.' Aisling gave her husband a look that said he would have to do some serious fecky brown-nosing to retain his husband of the year status.

'I'll have moussaka too,' Quinn said, eager to begin scoring brownie points, he added, 'And, I'll let you try some, Ash. I'll order a dessert, too, so you can have your own and share mine.'

Noah's voice rang out loud and clear once more, 'Bobby-Jean, I have a gerbil called Stef whose name used to be Steve.'

Ah, dear God, no! Maureen leapt in, 'Sure, now Bobby-Jean doesn't want to be hearing about gerbils, Noah.'

'No, you don't, do you Bobby-Jean?' Roisin quickly stepped in to avert a difficult conversation, willing Bobby-Jean to play ball. 'Here, Noah, have a roll.' She picked up the breadbasket and stuffed it in her son's mouth as if it were a ball, and he was one of those rotating clown heads at a fair.

'Au contraire Roisin, Maureen. I'd love to hear about your gerbils, Noah. I had a pet hamster when I was younger called Tallulah.' Bobby-Jean glanced at the others, all listening to the conversation, anxious to see how it would play out. 'You know, like Tallulah from Bugsy Malone? 'My Name is Tallulah'.' He sang the last part.

'You gals loved that film,' Bea jumped in. 'They used to tussle something terrible over who would marry Scott Baio when they grew up?'

'Pat's got the same dark eyes as Scott Baio,' Cindy batted her lashes at her fiancé.

Sherry stared hard at Pat. 'I beg to differ, Cindy. Scott's Italian. He looks Italian. Patrick's Irish. They don't look anything alike.'

'They do too.'

'Don't.

'Do.'

'Nope.' Sherry crossed her arms across her chest, and Cindy did the same. It was an impressive sight.

Bea clapped her hands. 'Simmer down now, you two. They're the best of friends or the worst of enemies.' Bea smiled around the table while her daughters glared at one another.

It was called being sisters, Maureen thought, looking at her offspring. Moira had been known to torment Aisling with Bono posters in her time aware Aisling was not a fan.

As Noah began speaking again, Maureen closed her eyes. Nobody could say she hadn't tried.

'Bobby-Jean, we all thought Steve was a boy until he had lots of baby gerbils, and that's when we realised, Mr Nibbles, that's my other gerbil, hadn't been sitting on him because he was a bully. He was sexing him. Steve was a girl. Are you like Steve? Did you become a Stef?'

Dear God in Heaven Above, out of the mouths of babes, Maureen thought.

Roisin had turned puce and was frantically apologising to Bobby-Jean for her son.

But, to Maureen's relief, Bobby-Jean was laughing uproariously. Cindy and Sherry looked equally amused, as did Bea and Big Jim. *As for Patrick, well*, she thought, *he was hard to read, but Pat had always been a man's man. Scratch that. He'd gone through a phase of being overtly interested in her pantyhose, but he'd come out the other side.*

Bobby-Jean's laughter petered off seeing the little boy's puzzled expression at what was so funny. 'Noah, I'm glad you asked me that question.'

Maureen cut Bobby-Jean off, going in for damage control. 'The thing is Bobby-Jean, what you need to understand is that we Irish are not as colourful as the Los Angeles people. Isn't that right?' she cast about the table.

'Speak for yourself, Mammy,' Moira said.

Trust Moira, she thought, carrying on with her explanation. 'That's not to say we're not open-minded people. Sure, my brother-in-law's a fashion designer with a very handsome boyfriend.'

Bronagh nodded effusively. 'I can vouch for that. I've seen the photographs.'

'Thank you, Bronagh.' Maureen thought she could always count on Bronagh, keen to make her point. 'But I can tell you that the likes of Venice Beach in Los Angeles were an eye-opener. 'Tis a sheltered life we've led in the Emerald Isle under the umbrella of the Catholic church. Ouch!' Maureen had received a kick in the shins from one of her daughters. It was probably Moira because she was hissing, 'Mammy,' and running her thumb and index finger across her mouth in a zip-it mime.

Bobby-Jean didn't look affronted, however, far from it. 'Maureen honey, it's perfectly fine. You don't need to explain yourself.'

'Neither do you, Bobby-Jean,' Roisin piped up across the table.

Bobby-Jean smiled at her. 'As I said, it's fine because, in my experience, it's better to be an open book right from the start. So, Noah, would you like me to butter that roll for you?'

'No, thank you. I'm a big boy.' Noah began massacring his roll, impatient for a reply.

Big Jim cleared his throat. 'Excuse me for interrupting. But I'll hold my hand up to being unsure of what to make of Bobby-Jean when Bea and I first met him or her, depending on the day. But I live and die by the motto that if you do right, by my children, my wife and me; I'll do right by you, and Bobby-Jean here's been a good friend to Cindy. So, that makes her alright by me. And I'm a very inclusive man,' Big Jim stated. 'I'm in politics. What is it you do, Doe-nell?'

'It's Donal, and er, I was in the electrics game,' Donal replied.

'And very good at it you were too, Donal,' Maureen supplied as she speared an olive, glad of the change in conversation. 'If you'd a faulty wire, Donal was your man. He's retired from work now but not from life.' Maureen's laugh was a little too high pitched. 'If you're planning a party and want a band to get everyone on the floor dancing, he's your man.'

Her daughters looked at her with alarm, but Maureen was on a roll, giving her son's soon-to-be in-laws and wedding celebrant her live-in manfriend's CV. 'Donal sings in a Kenny Rogers tribute band. Very good he is too, and I play tambourine.'

Big Jim slapped a meaty hand to his forehead. 'I knew you reminded me of someone.'

'Kenny Rogers! I can see the resemblance,' Bea exclaimed.

Donal launched into an impromptu few lines from The Gambler, with everyone around the table clapping along.

Maureen wasn't to be left out. 'Of course, I duet with Donal. You know the Dolly and Sheena songs. We also belong to many groups and keep ourselves very busy helping out with the grandbabies, too, don't we, Donal?'

'We do, Mo.'

'And you say you're not used to colourful people?' Bobby-Jean raised an expertly pencilled brow before addressing the Irish contingent with a sombre expression that didn't gel with the dazzling makeup and outfit. 'My name's Bobby-Jean, and I'm a cross-dresser.'

Was it like the AA meetings she'd seen on the television programmes? Maureen wondered. *Were they supposed to applaud?*

Cindy broke into peals of giggles. 'Bobby-Jean, you're so funny.'

Maureen failed to see the joke, and now she was in the dark like poor Noah. 'Is a cross-dresser the same as a transvestite?' she asked, wanting to be clear on the matter because she was far from an authority on the topic, but she had seen the Rocky Horror Picture Show, so she did know a thing or two.

'Mammy! We don't use that word anymore,' Roisin admonished. 'I'm sorry Bobby-Jean. Like she said, she's led a sheltered life.'

Maureen bristled, 'I said us Irish had led a sheltered life. I don't recall you stepping out with any of the transvestites, either. And, now that I think about it, I've decided to retract that statement because I've swingers for neighbours, and I live in sin with Donal. So if that doesn't make me liberal, I don't know what will.'

'But I still don't understand.' Noah wanted answers.

'To put it simply, Noah,' Bobby-Jean said gently. 'I have boy parts, and I like having boy parts. I also like girls very much. So much so that I like dressing in their clothes and wearing makeup sometimes. It makes me feel good. I've got the best of both worlds and am not too fond of labels. I'm just me.'

Noah puckered his lips as he did when mulling something over. 'I'm just me, too, but I don't think I'd like to wear girls' clothes.'

'I'm not saying it's for everyone,' Bobby-Jean said.

'But sometimes I'd like to be a girl because they don't seem to get told off us as much as the boys at school, and I would like to be able to feed babies like a cow when I grow up, but I don't like pink much and most girls I know like pink.'

Everybody around the table was laughing now.

Maureen studied Bobby-Jean's eyebrows. 'You've done an excellent job of your eyebrows there. Mine are getting a little thin, and I'm not very good at pencilling in. You were saying you're a makeup artist?'

'It's true she's not good with the pencil,' Moira butted in before Bobby-Jean could reply. 'She looks like Groucho Marx by the time she's finished drawing in pretend eyebrows.'

'Girls, let me tell you, Bobby-Jean here is worth her weight in gold regarding hair and makeup tips.' Bea cooed giving her bouffant a pat.

Cindy and Sherry, their earlier bickering forgotten, fluffed their white-blonde hair and agreed.

'And my lips are getting very mean-like,' Bronagh said.

'She outlines them with pencil outside her lip-line, Bobby-Jean, making her look like she's four lips,' Moira informed the jack-of-all-trades sitting next to her mammy.

'What you want to do, Maureen, Bronagh, is this—' Bobby-Jean said.

And just like that, they were away.

Chapter Fifteen

♥

'Actually, Mammy, I think you'll find the Catholic church is very open-minded these days,' Aisling informed Maureen in response to her query as to what the church would make of a heavily pregnant Cindy being married by a celebrant who enjoyed wearing both men's and women's clothes. 'They've had to move with the times.'

'Hmm, I think Father Fitzpatrick might have missed the decree.'

Mammy and daughter were poolside at the pension relaxing after a long, leisurely and, in the end, surprisingly enjoyable lunch. Maureen had warmed to Big Jim and Bea as the wine flowed; they were salt of the earth sort of people and Patrick could do a lot worse when it came to in-laws, she'd decided. She'd warm to Bea all the more though if she'd stop being so touchy feely with Donal, and she'd be sure to sit beside him at dinner tonight.

Aisling was snuggling Aoife, clad in a singlet top and nappy in her arms while Maureen bounced an identically dressed Connor on her knee receiving a gummy grin for her efforts that made her smile and coo. The umbrellas in their plastic stands shaded them from the sun which was only moderately less intense now that four o'clock had rolled around. There was a teasing whiff of meat grilling wafting on the air and underpinning it a sweet smell, like honeysuckle. *It must be the bougainvillea*, Maureen decided, admiring the vibrant hue.

Bronagh and Leonard were huddled up together on the sun loungers on the opposite side of the pool in which Noah was splashing about with his Poppa D. Maureen risked a glance at the couple who were as smitten as a pair of teenagers in love for the first time. They were a good match, although there was no need for Leonard to leave those socks and sandals of his on now they were making the most of the pension's pool. They couldn't carry on as they were, she mused. What with him in Liverpool and Bronagh in Dublin. Her money was on an engagement announcement in the not-too-distant future. First though, they'd a wedding to get through. Maureen envisaged Cindy in a white version of today's mini dress saying her vows, and broke out in a hot sweat.

'Watch Nana, watch!' Noah shouted. Donal had hold of him and Maureen laughed as he picked the little boy up, lifting him high before tossing him in the air. He screamed his delight in the split second before he splashed down in the pool. He emerged spitting out a mouthful of water, 'Again, Poppa D! Do it again!'

'Watch your back Donal!' Maureen called over then, seeing Moira splayed out three sun loungers down smirking, said, 'Don't.' Her daughter was glistening with so much oil as she worked on her tan that she'd have sizzled if tossed on a barbeque.

'Don't what?' Moira asked innocently, reaching for her bottle of tanning oil.

'Be mentioning the slipping hand massages. And I hope you know you're basting yourself with that stuff. It's the sunscreen like your sister you should be slapping on. Mark my words Moira O'Mara, you'll be a raisin by the time you're my age.'

Moira's attention was diverted by Tom saying, 'Wave to Mammy, Kiera!' She forgot the oil and waved back at her daughter who was wearing a pair of fluorescent orange arm bands being floated about by her daddy.

Absent from the poolside tableau was Quinn. He'd gone for an afternoon siesta. Roisin and Shay had also announced they were going for a rest. Moira had made the inverted commas fingers sign as they took their leave calling out, 'Enjoy your rest'. She'd received a slap from Mammy who told her to get her mind out the gutter which was why she opted to sunbathe out of reach from her now.

A shadow fell across Maureen and she shaded her eyes looking up. 'Hello there Georgios.'

'Maureen, I am so sorry to hear you have had an accident. I have just had a telephone call from Konstantinos to say you fell off the mule you were riding. Are you alright?' Concern flickered in his warm brown eyes.

'Sure, I'm grand so long as I have the cushion under me like so,' she pointed to the pink travel neck pillow she'd commandeered from Roisin at Tom's suggestion. He'd said it wasn't dissimilar to a post-pile surgery, care cushion and would help with her bruised bottom. Roisin had been reluctant to hand it over initially, saying that she'd never be able to use it again because she wasn't going to be able to put it around her neck after it having been under her mammy's arse. Maureen had reminded her as to who it was would be keeping an eye on her son while she and Shay went up to their room for a 'rest'. Roisin knowing which side her bread was buttered on had dutifully fetched the cushion.

Georgios smiled and said he was glad it was nothing too serious. 'May I sit?' He indicated the empty sun lounger and at Maureen's insistence he do just that, he sat down on the side of it angled towards her and Connor. The baby boy was babbling happily. 'And what would this little man's name be?' The twins had yet to be introduced to Georgios properly.

'This is Connor, and that's his sister Aoife over there. They're Aisling and Quinn's twins.'

Aisling waved Aoife's little hand over at them. Georgios waved back.

'You are happy with everything at Wendy's?'

'It's grand. We've been made very comfortable and welcome, so. She's a lovely woman.'

'She is.' Georgios nodded pleased. He'd pass this on to his good friend later.

Maureen was gesturing to the pool. 'And you've met Kiera. She's Kiera with a 'K' not a 'C'. And Noah there's having a whale of a time with his Poppa D.'

The little girl was certainly happier than she had been earlier, Georgios thought, watching her smiles of delight as her father played with her. If he were to close his eyes, he knew he'd see himself and Obelia. He wouldn't close his eyes though and allow himself to revisit those happier days because it would only lead to dwelling on how his middle years had turned out so differently to how he'd thought they would. Instead, he concentrated on the here and now, waggling his fingers and smiling as the baby boy grasped hold of his littlest finger with his tiny, dimpled hand.

Maureen watched on, smiling herself. You couldn't help but smile where the babbies were concerned.

'You are a lucky woman, Maureen, to have such a fine family around you.'

'I count my blessings every single day, Georgios. My grandchildren are a wonderful reward for the girls turning me grey before my time.

I've another one on the way too. My son who's getting married here in Santorini is expecting a baby shortly after Christmas. Well not him as such, his fiancée Cindy but you know what I mean. Of course, I'd have preferred them to wait to start a family until after they were married but your children have minds of their own. I always say being a mammy or a daddy is easy until the day they learn to say no.'

Georgios chortled his agreement but his eyes were tempered with sadness.

'Don't believe a word of what she's after telling you Georgios apart from Patrick and Cindy having a baby, that's true but as for me, Moira and Roisin. We were angels.' Aisling contradicted her mammy with a wink over at Moira. 'Weren't we Moira?'

'Angels,' Moira confirmed. 'Halos and everything.'

'Very skew-whiff halos.' Maureen butted back. 'Of course, I've even more blessings to be counting with Donal there.'

'Your husband.' Georgios wished he'd counted his blessings more with Ana. If he'd known he would lose her so soon, he would never have been too busy to just sit and talk. All the trivial things that had to be done like cleaning the pool or giving the pension a lick of paint, they could have all waited.

'Oh no, we're not married. He's my live-in manfriend. I was married at a young age to Brian, the girls and Pat's father, and a very happy union we made too but he died. It was the cancer that took him and his death left us all heartbroken. The young ones though they've their whole lives ahead of them to live and they find a way through the pain but Brian was my whole life. We'd been together longer than we'd been apart and it was very hard.' Maureen swallowed hard at the memories of that time. 'I handed the reins of the guesthouse we'd run together all our married life to Aisling and moved to the seaside. The girls thought I was mad but I needed a fresh start you see and I forced myself to try new things like learning to sail and line dancing. And then when I wasn't looking, along came Donal.'

Georgios was listening to the little Irish women intently and when she'd finished talking, he said quietly. 'I lost my Ana to cancer.'

Maureen reached over with her free hand and patted his. 'Tis a terrible disease and I'm very sorry to hear that. Do you have children?'

'A daughter, Obelia. She lives in Athens.' A shadow passed over his face.

Connor was beginning to fuss and Maureen, sensing Obelia was a thorny topic, jiggled her grandson and said, 'The best thing about grandchildren, Georgios, is you can hand them over to their own mammy and daddy whenever the mood takes you.' Accordingly, she hefted Connor across to Aisling who now had her hands full.

'How was your luncheon?' Georgios asked once Maureen had settled back in her lounger. It was in an obvious change of subject.

Aisling smirked getting in first over the top of Connor's protests. 'I'd say colourful is a good way to describe it.' She lay Aoife next to her on the lounger so as she could jig Connor up and down. He burped and instantly stopped fretting. 'There's a good boy.' She kissed him on the forehead and then told Georgios all about Bobby-Jean.

Georgios's thick eyebrows shot up into his hairline listening to Aisling, and Maureen supposed he wasn't used to colourful people either. She took over the conversation. 'I have to say though Georgios. Once you see past the whole boy parts wearing a wig and makeup thing, Bobby-Jean is a very nice person and if it couldn't be Father Fitzpatrick from St Theresa's, the church Patrick and the girls attended growing up marrying himself and Cindy, then Bobby-Jean will do nicely. At the end of the day, it's Patrick and Cindy's day, no one else's and if they're happy then I'm happy.'

'Jaysus Mammy, have you been on the sauce? Can I get that in writing in case Tom and I decide to make things legal, like?' Moira asked.

'No, I haven't and no, you can't.'

'I don't remember you being so free and easy when it came to my wedding arrangements, Mammy,' Aisling said.

'Girls are different,' Maureen said in a 'I'll be saying no more on the subject' manner.

Georgios pondered what Maureen had said about wanting her son and his future wife to be happy because it had hit a sore point. He wanted nothing more than for Obelia to be happy. It was his and Ana's dearest wish that this should be so but what he couldn't understand was why she couldn't be happy here. Santorini was her home. It was where she belonged. Why did she want to live far away from all that she'd known? He knew too if Obelia refused to be married by a priest, Ana would turn in her grave. 'Did you ask your priest if he would come to Santorini?' Georgios enquired, curious.

'No as it happened. The wedding was all very last minute because of the baby being on the way, like, and Patrick and Cindy had already decided they wanted Bobby-Jean to marry them.' Maureen thought about her portly priest and was quite certain had she dangled a free trip to Santorini under Father Fitzpatrick's nose, he'd have been hitching up his cassock and skipping down the beach in his papal slippers to marry the pair of them.

'If you're asking my opinion on lunch today—' Moira pulled herself upright on the lounger and pushed her glasses on top of her head.

'Nobody is asking your opinion Moira,' Maureen was quick to reply, wishing her daughter would wear a sensible bathing suit like her own. She'd long since given up on asking her daughters to cover their bits and bobs properly. Where they got their exhibitionist streak from, she didn't know.

Moira ignored her. 'I would describe lunch as colourful *and* entertaining. Cindy's accent's softened a little with living in LA but her family sound so funny. Donal's, Doe-nell, Mammy here is Mo-reen and when Sherry asked if there was any chance of fried chicken and slaw having been accidentally left off the menu, slaw rhymed with whore.'

Georgios found it amusing that the family with their sing-song way of talking should pass remark on another's accent.

Maureen told Moira not to use nasty words like so even though privately she had to agree. She'd overheard the conversation. Bea had clucked and said to Donal, 'She's never been any different. She was a fussy child and now she's a fussy adult. All she'll eat is fried chicken, potato mash and gravy with a side of slaw. I sometimes wonder if they swapped babies on me at the hospital and I've been raising Colonel Sanders' granddaughter all these years.'

'That wasn't the worst of it though, Georgios,' Moira said. 'We'd only just ordered when Noah shrieked, "Yuck!"'

Maureen zoned Moira out as she cringed, recalling how all eyes had flown to the little boy in time to witness a black bullet whizzing across the table. It hit Sherry smack bang in the middle of her forehead then bounced off to land on a white plate where it rolled around for a second.

Sherry blinked her surprise and rubbed the spot on her forehead.

'I thought it was a grape!' Noah wailed as his mother, realising he'd spat an olive across the table, was torn between giving him a telling off or consoling him.

She did neither and turned her attention to Sherry sitting there with a bewildered expression as to what had just happened on her face and apologised. 'Sure, you know yourself what it's like when you're expecting a burst of lovely, sweet grape in your mouth and you get a dishwash, salty olive instead?'

Moira made a strangled noise and the focus around the table moved from Sherry and the olive to her.

'Are you alright? Is she alright? She's not choking, is she?' Bea looked at Moira's mother and sisters with alarm.

It was all too much and a bubble of laughter escaped Moira's lips. Maureen was aghast but Big Jim began to shake too and then Bea joined in and Bobby-Jean's unexpected snort set them all off and soon they were wheezing with laughter around the table, even Sherry.

Noah was quite pleased with the effect he'd had on everyone but Roisin moved the olive bowl away from him lest he get any ideas about a repeat performance.

As Moira finished retelling the tale, Georgios too was laughing.

'And what are your plans for later?' he asked wiping his eyes.

Maureen spoke up. 'All the family are going for a meal in Oia to chat over the finer points of the wedding service.' Big Jim had said the restaurant he'd booked had come highly recommended and that it was the perfect location for viewing the island's famed sunset. He was insistent it was his and Bea's treat. She and Donal had protested of course and she'd ignored Moira standing on her foot yet again. But she was learning when Big Jim had made his mind up, he'd made his mind up. Now she reinforced to her girls that they were not to be greedy and order the entrées given someone else was going to be footing the bill.

'Don't forget we're meeting Cindy before dinner so we can try on our bridesmaids' dresses,' Aisling said.

'That should be interesting.' Moira leaned back in her lounger eager to soak up some more rays.

It was true, Maureen mused. It would be interesting because they'd not seen any pictures. Cindy had wanted to keep her wedding and bridesmaids' dresses as a surprise. She'd wear her sunflower dress and get Bobby-Jean's opinion on the print. Her new friend had promised to show her how to feather her brows with the eyebrow pencil too and assured Bronagh she'd teach her how to create luscious lips. Leonard's chicken kebab had gone down the wrong way hearing this and Bronagh had to pat him forcefully on the back. 'And what about yourself there, Georgios? What are your plans?' she asked, aware their host was still sitting with them.

'I shall go across to Wendy for dinner. We are both widowed and it suits us to eat together. We take it in turns to cook. She's been a very good friend to me.'

'And you to her, I dare so.' Maureen smiled, wondering if he was aware he was in love with his neighbour. It was evident in the softening of his face as he said her name. She'd only met Wendy briefly when she'd seen them off this morning but wondered whether the feeling was mutual. She didn't get to turn this one over in her mind because Noah had just run over and begun shaking himself off like a dog spraying her, Georgios and Aisling in droplets of water.

'Noah!' she admonished, chucking him the towel.

Georgios laughed as he stood up. Then, stretching said, 'Excuse me.'

'Nana?'

'Yes Noah?'

'What are Bobby-Jean's boobies made of?'

Janey Mack, Maureen thought. She could just picture the lad standing up in front of class at his new school when he got home and the teacher asked him to tell them all about his holiday to Greece.

Chapter Sixteen

♥

The shuttle ride back to Oia shortly after five that evening was bone-rattling, and they were all half deaf by the time they arrived from the Bouzouki and Syrtaki instrumental their driver, Yannie, had blaring. Leonard had put his hand in his pocket and paid their fare, rendering him the man of the moment. He'd even tipped the driver without being told to by Bronagh.

Maureen thought they'd arrived at the wrong resort as they all piled back into Azure Waters because the Bobby-Jean who put her drink down and got up from the sofa to greet them was not the same Bobby-Jean of earlier. This new version was a beachy-waves, blonde. There was no mistaking the six-foot frame and broad shoulders, though.

Air kissing ensued, and compliments on Bobby-Jean's blonde bombshell look.

'It looks grand on you alright, Bobby-Jean, but blonde's not for me.' Bronagh patted the jet-black bobbed hair she'd favoured for as long as anyone could remember. 'I bleached my hair in the days of Diana Dors, but I looked more like your Muppets' frog than screen siren. I cried for a week.'

Leonard gave his lady love's hand a sympathetic squeeze.

'It turned green?' Moira asked.

'Green,' Bronagh affirmed. 'My mam went berserk, so she did, ranting on that it served me right because if the good Lord had meant for me to be blonde, I'd have been born blonde.'

'I'm all for helping nature,' Bobby-Jean winked.

'Well, I, for one, love it,' Maureen stated, admiringly looking up at her new friend. 'I think I prefer it to the red. But, do you know, I've often wondered what I might look like as a blonde?'

'Dolly Parton without the bosoms,' Moira smirked.

'Shirley Temple in heels,' Aisling snickered.

They looked to Roisin expectantly.

'Erm, Jessica Rabbit with an Irish accent.'

'Very good.' Aisling and Moira gave their sister a pat on the back.

'Didn't she have red hair?' Shay asked, but no one answered because Donal had begun crooning, 'Just the Way you Are.'

'He's more Kenny than Billy Joel,' Moira whispered to Tom, who had Kiera hanging off him as she tried to grab Bobby-Jean's curls.

Noah stared fixedly at Bobby-Jean's chest and received a nudge from his mum.

Maureen didn't seem to mind Donal's tune, though, as she reassured her live-in manfriend she'd not be trading her brunette for bottle-blonde any time soon.

'Cindy tasked me with the meet and greet,' Bobby-Jean explained, then, checking the coast was clear, lowered her husky voice. 'Anyway, Bea, Cindy and Sherry are in the honeymoon suite waiting for us ladies. And Big Jim and Patrick are on the veranda enjoying a cheeky apéritif and pre-dinner nibbles.'

'Grand. Have fun, ladies,' Donal said, taking his leave while Quinn turned the pram toward the veranda as did Tom, the pushchair Kiera was strapped in. Noah took hold of Shay's hand, and Leonard followed after them. Meanwhile, Aisling had reacted like a dog would to the word 'walk' upon hearing there were nibbles nearby, and she'd been quick to ask if the ladies would be getting some, too, as she was breastfeeding two babbies and needed to eat regularly.

'Leave it with me, Aisling. I can't have you fading away on my watch.' Bobby-Jean, magnificent in a mauve maxi dress with spaghetti straps, turned her silver sandals toward the front desk and spoke quietly with Petra, who was still on duty. Then beckoning the remainder of their Irish party to follow her, she swayed off down the labyrinth of carved caves to tap on the door of room 16.

'Sixteen's Cindy's lucky number. It's why she asked for a set of 16 Gs when she had her,' Bobby-Jean winked and cupped her faux bosoms giving them a jiggle, 'done.'

'I knew they weren't what God gave her,' Moira whispered to Aisling and Roisin.

'I wonder if Bea's had hers done too,' Aisling replied as the door was flung open, and the woman herself was standing there.

'Evening, y'all!' Bea's hair nearly reached the door frame, and she was dressed for dinner. A vision in powder blue. *She was a woman who believed in matching her colours*, Maureen thought, taking stock of the blue eyeshadow, mascara and, with a glance down at her shoes, blue sling-backs. The welcoming kiss they each received, filing forth one by one, left a lipstick mark on the cheek akin to a nightclub entry stamp on the wrist.

'Isn't this lovely?' Maureen said, surveying the plush, spacious suite with a private balcony her son and his fiancée were booked into. The doors leading outside were framed by soft muslin drapes seeming to sigh in and out along with the gentle sea breeze.

Bronagh agreed with her sentiment while Moira's eyes were out like organ stoppers once more as she swept the elegant surroundings.

'I wonder if the sheets are Egyptian cotton or silk? My money's on Egyptian cotton.'

'You haven't got any money,' Aisling pointed out. 'Unlike Pat. He's got money to burn to stay in a place like this,' Aisling muttered to no one in particular and this time, Maureen pretended she hadn't heard her.

Even Roisin, who didn't have a materialistic bone in her body, could appreciate the romance of the room.

'Cindy's doing her makeup with Sherry in the bathroom,' Bea explained as she pulled a bottle of Bollinger from the ice bucket. 'Champagne girls?' *Girls sounded like gals*, Maureen thought, and Bea, not waiting for an answer, headed for the balcony, where she expertly popped the cork.

'You've done that before,' Roisin laughed, holding the flute she'd picked up off the tray out as Bea approached her.

'Orange juice for me, please, Bea,' Aisling said, looking longingly at the bubbles. 'I'm breastfeeding for two.'

There was a collective eye-rolling amongst her sisters, Mammy and Bronagh.

'And, for me,' Moira added, dragging her eyes from the glass of golden fizz Roisin was holding. 'I'm not breastfeeding. Heaven forbid, size of my daughter's teethy-pegs these days. I choose to abstain.'

'Good for you, sugar.' Bea sloshed juice in a glass.

Maureen looked on as Moira accepted the drink. She was proud of her. Moira had decided to stay off the sauce and stuck to it. There had been times, like now, when the temptation to indulge must be strong, but she held firm. *Her daughter's determination might drive her demented at times*, Maureen thought, accepting a glass of the good stuff herself as did Bronagh, but it had stood her in good stead.

Bea filled her glass and raised it. 'I'll keep this short, sweet and straight to the point. To Patrick, Cindy and us. A brand-new family.'

The sentiment echoed around the room.

'Here, here.' Maureen leaned over and clinked her glass. She took a lusty sip, in the mood for celebrating because there was plenty to celebrate. They were here. Against all odds and with a lot of help from Bronagh, they'd made it to Santorini. She gave Bronagh's glass a thank-you tap.

Sherry's head bobbed around the bathroom door. 'Mom, can you give us a hand with Cindy's gown?'

Maureen remembered what they were here for. A glimpse of what the bride-to-be would be wearing in a few days' time when she exchanged vows with Patrick on the beach. She steeled herself for a peek at the inevitable barely-there bridal whatever.

'Excuse me, y'all. Bea set her glass down and bustled into the bathroom.

Gown? Sherry had said gown. Not swimsuit or minidress? Maureen thought with hope shining through. She glanced down at her frock and then at Bobby-Jean's dress. Her former reservations over the floral print Ciara had done the hard sell on floated back to the fore. Bronagh had told her she looked very well in it, but she'd said it in a high-pitched voice. Now she wished she'd opted for something plain like Bronagh's. Perhaps not quite as tight as her pencil dress with capped sleeves, though. She'd ask Bobby-Jean's opinion as planned, she decided.

'Bobby-Jean, what do you think of my dress?' Maureen twirled, and then, coming full circle, she struck a hands-on-hips pose. The bubbles had made her a little giddy, as had the twirling, and it took a second or two for her head to catch up with her body. 'Ciara with a 'C' assured me it would be a versatile Santorini holiday wardrobe staple and that I could dress it up like so.' She kicked her ankle out to show the strappy white summer sandals she was risking life and limb by wearing given the cobbled laneways she'd no doubt be tackling on her way to dinner. 'Or down, with flats in the daytime.'

Bobby-Jean appraised Maureen pensively, tapping a pale pink-painted fingernail to matching lips, 'Can we be honest with each other, Maureen?'

'Honesty's the best policy, Bobby-Jean, and you can call me Mo.'

'That means she likes you Bobby-Jean,' Moira supplied from where she was lounging on Cindy and Patrick's bed, her orange juice in hand. Her sisters were perched on the end of the bed, enjoying their drinks.

'Bobby-Jean's quite the mouthful,' Maureen said. 'Maybe I could call you BJ instead?'

Moira coughed on her OJ and spluttered, 'No, you can't be calling her BJ, Mammy!'

'And since when was your name Bobby-Jean or BJ, for that matter?' Maureen shot across the room to Moira. 'And don't be lounging on the matrimonial bed like so.'

'I hadn't thought of that,' Moira said, screwing her face up as she righted herself and squished up alongside her sisters at the foot of the bed instead. 'And, I'm sorry Bobby-Jean, but we already told you Mammy's innocent. An innocent who loves abbreviations. It's embarrassing, so it is. And will you tell her the dress makes her look like one of those dancing flower gimmicks, only without the pot?'

'She's right, Mammy,' Roisin and Aisling nodded from their perch on the end of the bed. 'It does.'

'Don't be rude to your mammy who loves you girls,' Bronagh butted in, but Moira was already telling Bobby-Jean about the orange dress Mammy had worn all summer.

'She was always going on about it being BO-coloured.'

'It was. BO. It stands for burnt orange. What's wrong with that?'
Maureen gave all three of her daughters a haughty glare. 'And when
I want your fashion advice, I'll ask for it, and I don't recall asking.'
She drew herself up to her full height of five feet, nothing not finished
yet, as she added, 'Not all of us want to get about showing our arses,
midriffs or with our bosoms threatening to break free. Some of us
prefer to look stylish and elegant. Isn't that right, Bronagh?'

'We do, Mo.'

'Or like a sunflower with a face,' Moira said under her breath, but
she did tug her skirt down her thighs a little while Aisling rearranged
her bosom, and Roisin rued, having chosen a bustier peasant blouse
and boho skirt.

Bobby-Jean stepped in. 'Mo, the girls have a point. I think maybe
Bo, as in Bo Derek, might be better. Or what about Bo-J? That's got a
certain ring to it.'

'Bo-J.' Maureen sounded it out. 'Now I like that, and Bo and Mo
rhymes.' Maureen clapped her hands delightedly. 'My middle name
starts with a 'C'. So you can call me Mo-C.'

'It sounds like a Gangsta rap handle, Mammy.' Aisling said, frowning. 'You might as well put a 'Lil' in front of it.'

'Lil Mo-C's in da house,' Roisin giggled loudly.

'There'll be no more of that,' Maureen pointed to the Bollinger
bottle on ice, 'If you start carrying on like so.'

Bronagh hustled into the conversation, 'And I can be Bro-T. 'T' for
Teresa.'

'Jaysus wept,' Moira groaned. 'Now you've got that sorted, Bo-J will
you tell Lil Mo-C what you think of the dress?'

Maureen stood to attention, waiting for the verdict.

'Okay. So, I think your stylist Ciara—'

'With a 'C',' Maureen butted in.

'With a 'C', had the right idea. It is a gorgeous dress, but the pattern is a little too busy for someone as petite as you.'

If any of her girls had told her this, Maureen would have taken umbrage, but the way Bobby-Jean dropped the word petite into the conversation took the sting away from having bought a dress that didn't suit her. So perhaps Ciara's word wasn't fashion gospel after all, and next time she needed a new dress, she'd be taking someone with her for a second opinion.

'I'd loan you something of mine, but we're not the same size,' Bobby-Jean said, pointing out the obvious. 'I played linebacker in my high school football days, and anything in my wardrobe would swamp you.'

'It's the thought that counts,' Maureen said.

'Don't worry, Mammy, it will be dark outside soon, and no one will be able to see your dress.' Aisling tried and failed to be helpful.

'Mo-C and Bro-T, what do you think about the three of us making a shopping date tomorrow morning?' Bobby-Jean asked. 'I saw some gorgeous boutiques in the village earlier today.'

'I'm always up for shopping, Bo-J,' Maureen said. 'And you're a proper stylist. Not like Ciara.'

'It's safe to say Ciara with a 'C' has been written out of the Will,' Moira said.

'There'll be no more cream cakes for her,' Aisling added with a smug smile.

'Count me in, too, Bo-J,' Bronagh added. 'I could do with a wardrobe overhaul.'

'Can I come, Mammy?' Moira asked, not wanting to miss out.

'No, you cannot.' Maureen was on to her youngest child. But, of course, she'd be expecting her to put her hand in her purse all morning, given she was a student and all.

Bea opened the bathroom door a crack. 'Okay, everyone, our bride's ready. Close your eyes now.'

Eyelids fluttered shut, and they heard a rustling sound, then Bea's voice, 'Okay, you can open them!'

Everybody did just that and stood blinking at the bridal apparition in front of them because it wasn't what they expected. Not at all.

Chapter Seventeen

♥

'What do you think?' Cindy asked, almost shyly, rustling her skirts as she stood framed in the bathroom doorway.

Maureen's hands had flown to her mouth because the dress Cindy had chosen was positively Amish by her usual standards. Oh, the relief the bride-to-be wasn't standing in front of her in a swimsuit like that American actress wan who'd tied the knot on the beach! The gown she'd opted for was pure white and full-length with a modest neckline and lace-capped sleeves. A satin bow sat beneath her enormous bust, but there was no hint of cleavage, and the fabric flowed discreetly over her baby bump. 'You look busty, er beautiful, Cindy. Your dress is, well, it's perfect,' Maureen said at last, dropping her hands and taking a step forward to kiss her.

Cindy flushed with pleasure at getting her future mother-in-law's stamp of approval.

'Thank you, Mom. I was worried you might not like it because it's not my usual style.'

Maureen was a little taken aback that her opinion should matter. Her girls never paid her any heed, so it was flattering that Cindy cared what she thought. The champagne made her effusive as she grasped the woman who would soon become her daughter-in-law by the hands. 'You're pretty as a picture, and Patrick will think himself the luckiest man in the world when he sees you like so. You two will have the happiest day of your lives on Friday. We'll all see to that. Won't we?' She looked around the room for confirmation.

There were nods and promises of 'We will.' Although as soon as their mammy's back was turned, the sisters looked at one other with raised eyebrows. Was this the same mammy who'd been going on about Cindy and Pat not having a church wedding?

Cindy was blinking back tears. 'I can't wait to be an O'Mara, Mom.'

Moira spoke up. 'And, we can't wait for you to be one, but the name comes with a warning, so listen up. Uncle Bartley. If you ever meet him and he offers you the cheese and crackers, don't eat them. And you look stunning, by the way.'

'Gorgeous,' Roisin breathed. 'I love your dress.'

'It's fabulous. You look fabulous.' Aisling smiled and then brought up an equally pressing matter. 'Do you think the snacks will be long, Bo-J?'

'I wondered what that rumbling noise was. I thought there must be a train line somewhere nearby,' Bronagh said.

'No, it was my tummy.'

Then, remembering Cindy was waiting for her to comment, Bronagh said, 'You're a storybook princess, so you are.'

'Girl, you are the bomb.' Bobby-Jean dabbed her eyes with a tissue hastily pulled from a box on the occasional table. 'Patrick's a lucky man. And Aisling, Petra said the platter would be fifteen minutes or so. So it should be on its way.'

For the first time since Cindy had come on the scene, Maureen found herself inclined to agree that Patrick had done well for himself. The photographs of her and Pat's big day would be wonderful. All her fears had been swept away, and she was already picturing herself passing the developed film packets around the line-dancing ladies.

'Would you look at Bea,' Moira whispered. 'She's puffed up like one of those fish they serve in Japanese restaurants. You know the Russian Roulette wans. Do you think she'll pop?'

'A puffer fish, and that's a proud mammy for you.' Roisin blinked back tears. She was the most sentimental of the sisters, although Aisling would say it was her.

Cindy swished her skirt from side to side, enjoying the attention. 'I'm not wearing shoes, of course, because it's on the beach and everybody's going to be barefoot. I mean, it's a beach wedding, after all,' she tittered.

'Of course. You couldn't be wearing shoes on the beach,' everybody tittered back but with a hint of anxiety. Where would they get an emergency pedicure between now and then? Maureen was especially worried because her heels were very dry. You couldn't have cracked heels in a wedding photo.

'I don't want to take the dress off.' Cindy swished some more. 'I feel like a Disney princess.'

'I don't blame you, but you don't want to mark it now before the big day, do you?' Maureen bossed.

'Mo-reen's right. Us Mommas know best.' Bea gave Maureen a conspiratorial wink.

'I wonder what we'll be wearing.' Aisling lowered her voice and addressed her sisters.

'My money's on strapless,' Moira replied.

'We already had that conversation, and you don't have any money. So, I'm going with chaste like a medieval lady in waiting,' Aisling butted back. 'And, I hate strapless anything. You know I don't get on with it.'

Moira snorted, earning herself a sharp glance from her mammy and the attention of Cindy, Bea, Bobby-Jean and Bronagh. 'That's right, I'd almost forgotten about that time we were clubbing, and you had a strapless dress on.'

'Alright, alright, you don't need to remind me thanks very much.'

Moira wasn't stopping now she had an audience. Between giggles, she relayed how Aisling's strapless bra had wound up slowly slipping down until it was round her middle like a hula-hoop while waving her arms about to Oasis's 'Wonderwall'. 'I'm in bits whenever that song comes on the radio.'

'It's an experience I've no wish to repeat,' Aisling muttered, glaring at the others as she dared them to laugh.

'Well, I think our dresses will be snugly fitted to offset Cindy's princessyness.' Roisin slurped the remainder of her fizz.

'Cindy, can I come out yet?' A plaintive voice sounded from the depths of the bathroom.

Cindy's mouth formed an 'O'. 'I forgot all about you, Sherry. She's doing the bridesmaid reveal! Come on out.'

Sherry hustled forth with a veil, going on about how her sister used to do the same thing when they played hide 'n' seek as kids.

Moira copping a load of peach-coloured corset top and matching tulle skirt, began humming 'Like a Virgin' under her breath.

'Suffice to say there's none of those in the room.' Maureen shot her youngest daughter a fierce look.

Bronagh moved to her friend's side in case she was in danger of swooning again.

Sherry pinned the veil to her sister's head with more force than necessary before striking a pose. 'Ta-dah!' She flung one arm in the air, and the other rested on her hip and Jaysus wept. Were they to put side bows in their teased hair and drape pearls and crosses around their necks too? All that was missing were fingerless gloves. Roisin, Aisling and Moira stared at one another in silent horror.

Maureen didn't like to say peach didn't do anything for Roisin and Moira's colouring. On the contrary, it made them look jaundiced. Nor was it the best on Aisling, leaving her looking like she'd been fighting off a tummy bug. Her girls just weren't peach girls.

Roisin, Aisling and Moira were saved from having to enthuse about Sherry's peach homage to the eighties by the bell. Literally.

Bea opened the door, and a young man stood there with a platter of bread and dips, which he was directed to leave on the table next to the champagne bucket. Bea gave him a generous tip, and as he left, he turned and looked at Cindy and Sherry. 'Do you have a fancy-dress party to go to tonight?' His English was excellent, and not waiting for an answer, he said, 'I think you will both win prizes.' He beamed and, pocketing his money, found the door hastily shut in his face.

Aisling swooped on the food. The shock was wearing off, and she didn't care what she wore so long as she got fed. 'The outfit's grand, Sherry,' she lied through a mouthful of hummus and pita bread. Then, she scooped up an interesting pink dip. 'Ooh, this one's nice. I wonder what it is.'

Bobby-Jean moved over and looked at the dipping bowl. Aisling was already going for seconds. 'That's taramasalata. It's made with fish roe.'

Aisling opted not to have thirds.

Sherry lowered her arm and addressed Roisin, Moira and Aisling. 'This is our bridesmaid dress; technically, it's not a dress. It's a corset and skirt. Isn't it dreamy? I feel so, so—'

'Virgin-like?' Moira supplied.

'Ethereal,' Sherry said as if she hadn't heard Moira's remark. 'When Cindy gave me my head bridesmaid's brief, she told me she wanted hers and Patrick's day to be about joyous expression. And I instantly thought, what could be more joyous than dancing to meet your soul mate before exchanging vows?'

Cindy jiggled with excitement. 'It's such a wonderful idea. I can't wait to see Patrick's face when we dance down the beach toward him.'

Neither could Maureen, and she knew if she could tune into her daughters' thoughts, they'd all be silently crying out, 'No!'

'Cindy's all-time favourite music artist is Madonna, and I'm a big believer in looking the part to play the part.' Sherry addressed the three O'Mara sisters and then did some fancy synchronised arm and footwork.

Maureen thought she was a woman after her own heart, vaguely recalling Sherry had said something about being a dance instructor at lunchtime.

'I've named the dance I've choreographed, 'Santorini Wedding', and I'm going to need you to set aside a couple of hours tomorrow afternoon to rehearse the steps.' Sherry's tone didn't invite any argument, but Moira boldly pulled a regretful face.

'I hate to tell you, Sherry, but I've two left feet. It might be better if we just trotted up the beach behind Cindy.'

'She does, and I'm as awkward as a cow on roller skates,' Aisling lamented, keeping quiet about her salsa dancing skills.

Roisin, the most naturally coordinated of the three, did not mention she was a yoga instructor as she said, 'It runs in the family, Sherry, the cow on roller skates thing. So, I'm with Moira. It would be better if we all just trotted down the beach. We don't want to be showing Cindy or yourself up like.'

'If I can get five-year-olds coordinated performing 'Thriller', then you three will be a walk in the park.' Sherry had a gritted teeth determination about her.

'Maybe we could just skip instead?' Aisling suggested, receiving an elbow in the ribs from both sisters.

'What music were you thinking of playing?' Maureen queried. She was familiar with Madonna's greatest hits and silently prayed it wouldn't be the 'Like a Virgin' wan, or else spectators would assume there'd been an immaculate conception where the bride was concerned.

'Cindy's all-time favourite Madonna song is 'Papa Don't Preach'.'

Ah no! That was worse. Not the song about the illegitimate babby! Maureen was aghast and would have to tell Donal not to bother with the camcorder at the ceremony if that was the case.

'That's my favourite too,' Bronagh jumped in unhelpfully.

Bronagh and Cindy launched into a few impromptu out-of-tune lines from the song while Bea and Bobby-Jean clapped. Maureen, Roisin, Aisling and Moira couldn't bring themselves to join in.

Sherry clapped her hands before they could sing the chorus for the second time. 'But given Cindy's bun in the oven, I didn't think it was appropriate.'

At last, Maureen thought, *the girl was speaking sense*, relieved Sherry wasn't going to run with a Madge instrumental after all.

'Soo...'

There was no drumroll.

'We settled on 'Into the Groove'.'

Roisin, Moira and Aisling looked from one to the other. Sherry wasn't joking. Before the week was out, they'd be getting into the groove on a public beach in Santorini.

Chapter Eighteen

Roisin was the first to pull herself together. Friday's wedding wasn't their day. It was Cindy's; if she wanted Madonna-dancing bridesmaids, so be it. As the oldest sister, her job was to rally her siblings. 'It's going to be so memorable, Cindy, Sherry.'

'Mm, memorable.' Aisling tried to jab enthusiasm into her tone.

'No one will ever forget it,' Moira added, forcing her mouth upwards at the corners.

Maureen gave them a gold star for effort. She could afford to be magnanimous, given she'd not have to learn any dances.

'Have we got time for the girls here to try their outfits on, Momma?' Sherry questioned Bea. 'I thought it might be a good idea for you to try them on before we head out for dinner. I mean, the dressmaker we used is excellent, and she had all their measurements, but it wouldn't hurt to make sure.'

'That's smart, Sherry. We don't need any disasters on the day,' Maureen said, and Aisling scooped up another dollop of hummus and stepped away from the platter reluctantly as her mammy told her to stop stuffing her face or she wouldn't get the corset's zipper up.

Aisling opened her mouth to argue, but Maureen held up her hand. 'You don't need to say it. We know you're feeding two babbies.'

'I can't wait to see them all together.' Cindy jiggled into the walk-in wardrobe to retrieve the remaining bridesmaids' outfits while Bea indicated the champers.

'Help yourselves. It'd be a crime to waste it.'

'It would, and I'm a law-abiding citizen,' Bronagh chuckled as she whipped the bottle out and filled up the glasses already angled toward her.

'A tad more, Bronagh,' Roisin urged as the bubbles splashed into her flute. 'Fortification, like.'

Cindy returned and laid three dry cleaning bag-covered items over the back of the dressing table chair. She whipped the plastic sheath off and inspected the tag inside the corset. 'I had Monica sew on your first initials. This is yours, Aisling.'

Aisling, walking like she was being sent to the gallows, took the corset and skirt from Cindy and padded into the bathroom as Cindy called Roisin over.

Then, as Moira filed into the bathroom after her sisters, Bronagh called, 'Don't mess about now, girls, we've only twenty minutes until dinner.'

'I'll get indigestion, rushing, Bronagh,' Aisling complained, closing the bathroom door. 'I hope I can breathe in this fecking thing.' She reached for the corset.

'At least we'll all look like eejits together. There's strength in numbers, and it's not as if it will be the first time,' Roisin said, stripping off as her sisters did the same. She stepped into the mound of tulle with its elasticated waist and then, holding the corset to her chest, turned her back toward them. 'Zip me up one of you, would you?'

Aisling obliged and then turned so Roisin could do the same for her.

'You'll have to breathe in, Ash.'

'I am! And don't pinch my back with that zip.'

'Moira, I might need your help,' Roisin said through clenched teeth. Her face, reflected in the mirror, was red with exertion.

Moira, who'd succeeded in doing herself up, rustled in behind Aisling to pull the fabric together so Roisin could inch the zip up bit by bit.

'Nearly there. Inhale, deep as you can now, Ash,' Roisin ordered.

Aisling sucked air in like she was about to do a deep-sea dive.

Roisin gave a triumphant cry. 'Got it!'

'Ah no!' Aisling wailed, turning this way and that in the mirror.

'What? You've not split the seams, have you?' Roisin asked, alarmed. There'd be hell to pay if she had. How would they find a dressmaker to let the corset out at such short notice?

'No, I have not. But look.' She turned side on to her sisters. 'I've four bosoms.'

'Tis true that. You do. But sure, look on the bright side, two for the babbies and two for Quinn. Win, win.' Moira stated, earning herself a thump from her sister.

'You're not funny,' Aisling said, looking close to tears. 'I'm like a big round fecking peach.'

'No, you're not Ash. You look like you were born to dance, so you do.'

'Rosi, that's overdoing it,' Moira said.

'A dancing big round fecking peach then. I'm going to feel such an arse.'

'You're not the only one,' Moira said, equally glum.

'Girls, we need a team talk,' Roisin said, pulling her sisters in next to her, taking her role as the eldest sister seriously. 'This is what Cindy wants, right?'

'Right,' Moira and Aisling agreed.

'And she's the bride, so shouldn't she have what she wants?'

'Not at our expense,' Moira pouted.

'Put yourself in Cindy's shoes. Imagine if your bridesmaids all had faces on them like slapped arses. How would you like it? Haven't we come all this way so she and Pat can have a day they'll remember for the rest of their lives?'

'You're right,' Aisling said, trying to push her bosoms back into the corset.

'We could always pretend we're after filming a music video or something. I suppose,' Moira said.

'That's better. And we don't look that bad.'

All their eyes fixed on the apparitions reflected at them.

'Rosi, we look like a mismatched ballet troupe about to thud on to stage to perform 'Swan Lake'.' Aisling couldn't suppress a grin seeing the funny side of things.

'We do.' Moira's posture and expression would have had any ballet teacher worth her salt telling her to lift her chin, elongate her neck and be more swan-like before she attempted an ungraceful pirouette.

Roisin laughed and began humming a familiar tune. Then, she leaned forward and snatched up the deodorant before giving Moira and Aisling a hip bump.

It got them going.

Moira grabbed a can of hairspray and Aisling a bottle of moisturiser. She quickly squizzed the label and smirked, seeing it was for men. Patrick utilised more beauty products than his sisters these days.

Roisin held her hand up to show she was still in charge, 'Okay, a one-a-two-a-one, two, three. four.'

They launched into 'Like a Virgin'.

By the time they reached the chorus, there was a rapping on the door. 'What's with all the caterwauling, and what's the holdup?' Maureen demanded.

'Nothing Mammy,' Roisin choked out before they collapsed against one another in a fit of giggles.

Chapter Nineteen

♥

Maureen had her arm linked through Donal's as they passed through the entrance of the busy taverna with its convivial atmosphere of garlicky smells, clinking glasses and the scrape of cutlery. Chatter and laughter mingled with soft traditional background music, and several waiters worked the room with welcoming smiles. *Bo-J was turning heads*, she thought, witnessing more than one diner in danger of whiplash. She couldn't catch a glimpse of the maître d' because Big Jim was blocking her view, but the woman who'd checked their reservation led them to an expansive terrace. Just like the infinity pool back at Cindy and Patrick's resort, it seemed to float between the sky and sea.

At this rate, Moira was in danger of dumping Tom for a Russian oligarch, Maureen thought, hearing her daughter go into raptures once more. However, she too was impressed as they were led to a table *which surely must be the best in the house*, she thought, glancing around to where a couple were gazing into one another's eyes at an intimate table for two and a smaller party were tucking into their meals as though they'd not eaten in days. 'You've done us proud, Big Jim,' she said approvingly.

'Best seat in the house, Maureen.' Big Jim echoed her thoughts as Donal pulled a seat out for her, and she sat down gingerly to face the uninterrupted view. She'd had a quiet word in his ear about keeping a safe distance from Bea.

'How's your bottom doing there, Mo-C?' Bronagh asked.

Maureen tested her weight out, lifting one cheek and then the other. 'It's not too bad, Bro-T. I'm glad I left the travel pillow back at the pension.'

'There's something to be said for having a bit of extra padding as you get older,' Bronagh said.

Speak for yourself, Maureen thought, muttering on about extra padding indeed while Big Jim commandeered the seat at the top of the table seat. Fair play to him, given he was footing the bill and was the bride's father. Tonight, as he began polishing his knife with a napkin, he was making Maureen think of the old Godfather movie, and she was relieved to see Bea was a safe distance away as she sat to his left, Sherry on his right. Roisin would have to keep an eye on Shay, though. Bea was already helping him arrange his napkin on his lap.

'Bags first,' Aisling shouted, just about flattening Moira, who had nipped into the last seat facing the Caldera.

'I was here first,' Moira wheezed.

'Don't be showing me up, you two,' Maureen warned. 'Aisling, get off your sister. She can't breathe.'

Aisling had to concede defeat because Moira wouldn't budge; besides, Quinn was already patting the seat next to him in invitation. He was down the opposite end of the table to Big Jim and co and had parked the pram beside him. Tom had disappeared inside the taverna to locate a high chair, and once Moira saw Aisling sit down, she decided it was safe to vacate her seat and unstrap Kiera from her pushchair.

Tom returned, carting a baby feeding chair that looked to be from the days of the arc. He slotted it between him and Moira, and Moira slid Kiera into it, buckling her in before giving her a spoon to bang while she waited for something to eat.

Once the kerfuffle of seating arrangements was sorted, Big Jim tapped the side of his glass with the gleaming knife to get their attention because a waiter had magically materialised beside him.

The young man holding a pen and pad cleared his throat, 'Good evening and welcome to The Athenian. I am your waiter for the evening, Jonas.'

'Hello there, Jonas.' Maureen called over with a waggle of her fingers.

'That's Mo-reen. She's the groom's momma. She's Irish,' Big Jim added as though that explained everything.

'*Kalispera,*' the waiter, who looked in his late twenties, nodded toward Maureen.

'That means good evening,' Donal whispered to his lady love.

Jonas began running through the specials. He could recommend the fish of the day, he informed them because barracuda happened to be the chef's speciality. Then, he passed out dinner menus and told them they'd find the drinks menus at the back.

Maureen snapped her menu open to the last page and perused the list. 'What's Retsina like?' she wondered out loud.

'Rocket fuel,' Quinn stated. 'Same as the Ouzo.'

Tom and Shay instantly joined him in swapping horrendous Ouzo hangover stories.

'Retsina wine to the Greeks is what Guinness is to the Irish,' Donal said, impressing Maureen once more with his knowledgeability. 'It's fermented with small amounts of pine resin, which I imagine gives it a turpentine sort-a taste.'

'But it's traditional Donal and when in Rome or rather Greece,' Maureen said before urging her manfriend to be adventurous. Sure, hadn't she had the moussaka for lunch? Nobody could say Maureen O'Mara was the sort of woman who went abroad and ordered a full Irish for breakfast, a toasted club sandwich for lunch and fish and chips for dinner. No, she prided herself on embracing the culture of the country she was visiting. Not that she'd been abroad much, which was another reason to squeeze every last drop of culture from her time here in Santorini. 'I'll have a glass of Retsina, please, Jonas.'

'Very good. It pairs well with seafood,' Jonas said before scribbling on his pad.

'I've been adventurous enough knocking back the pre-dinner Ouzo aperitifs with Big Jim and the rest of the lads here while we waited for you ladies to rejoin us, Mo. That's quite enough culture for one night. I'll have a glass of your house red there, Jonas. Thanks.'

'Here, here,' Leonard said to Donal before calling out to Jonas. 'I'll have the same as him, thanks.'

Bronagh, who'd also not had the luxury of travel much in her sixty-plus years, was feeling adventurous and had decided to join Maureen in a glass of the Greek wine.

Jonas finished taking their orders and left them to peruse their dinner options.

Maureen skimmed over the six mains on offer.

Patrick was telling Cindy he preferred a menu with fewer dishes because when there were pages and pages to choose from, he always struggled to make his mind up and was invariably disappointed by his choice.

Maureen found this comment amusing because from what she'd witnessed dining out with the couple, it was Cindy who usually made his choices for him based upon whatever dietary fad was currently hot in Los Angeles. Thank goodness the pair of them seemed to be enjoying eating like everybody else this time around. Pregnancy suited Cindy.

Shay spoke up from where he was sandwiched between Noah and Quinn, 'The fewer items on a menu means the more chance of them being done well. The scallops and pasta sound good.'

Roisin leaned around Noah to murmur her agreement.

Quinn was quick to agree in his capacity as a chef and restaurant owner that it was better to specialise in a few dishes and do them exceptionally well rather than offer pages of choice and serve average meals.

'So what you're saying is a chef shouldn't be a jack-of-all-trades,' Leonard summed up.

'Exactly, Leonard. The ingredients are seasonal, too, and the fish caught today. You can't go wrong.'

Maureen scanned the page. It all sounded delicious, and she might have to close her eyes and jab at the menu randomly to make her mind up. 'What are you having, Bo-J?'

'I'm leaning toward the scallops,' Bobby-Jean said, eyes visible above the menu she was holding up. 'What about you, Mo-C?'

'Jaysus wept,' Moira mumbled.

'I'm not sure yet, Bo-J.' Then, they both went back to studying the menus.

Donal was listening to Patrick talk about his latest business venture, so Maureen leaned toward Bronagh. She was in a deep confab with Leonard as to what the time would be in Dublin after dinner if they were to telephone Bronagh's mam, Myrna, to see how she and Joan were getting on.

Maureen thought it was very kind of Leonard's sister, Joan, to volunteer to come and stay with Bronagh's dear old mam for the week.

She was fond of Myrna, whose health hadn't been good for years, and while she had a caregiver who called in every day to check on her, it was leaving her alone in the evenings Bronagh had fretted about. She'd asked her sister if she would come and stay with their mam for the week she'd be in Santorini, but it wasn't convenient. It had made Maureen's blood boil when Bronagh confided her sister was going on her annual holiday to Spain that week and couldn't possibly cancel it to look after their mam. All the sacrifices Bronagh had made over the years!

It was Bronagh who'd cared for Myrna ever since she'd first become poorly, sacrificing her chance for love for the sake of her mam, but then she'd begun seeing Leonard. Leonard didn't see Myrna as competition for Bronagh's affections; her friend had taken on a new lease of life as her romance blossomed. *She and Bronagh were proof you were never too old when it came to matters of the heart,* she thought, glancing fondly at Donal.

Bobby-Jean was swapping makeup tips with Moira, and Big Jim was bending Tom's ear about an ingrown toenail in a booming voice, given Tom was three seats away from him. The loved-up couple dining nearby also seemed intent on hearing Tom's advice.

Bea told Shay he bore an uncanny resemblance to the men on the covers of the romantic novels she devoured. He only needed to don a cowboy hat and whip off his shirt. Roisin was looking alarmed hearing this, and poor Noah was in danger of being crushed as she moved her seat closer to her man.

Aisling was chatting to Cindy about maternity bras while Quinn gently rocked the pram with his foot.

Maureen's attention was diverted as an almost full-to-the-brim, wide-lipped frosty wine glass was placed on the table before her. 'Thanks a million,' she said, eyes alighting on the golden liquid.

'Tis a lovely golden colour, Bronagh, and I'm giving the bartender full marks for his generous pour. Tis nothing like the mean little puddle of wine that barely covers the bottom of your glass they're so fond of serving up in Howth and the likes.'

'It tis indeed a decent glass, Maureen,' Bronagh agreed, eyeing hers greedily. 'And Jonas said it pairs well with seafood, so I'm considering ordering the steamed mussels. They sound delicious, and the mussels are very low in carbohydrates and good for the libido, Maureen.'

'But they're soaked in Ouzo and cream, Bronagh,' Moira pointed out, 'and I think you're mixing mussels with oysters.'

Bronagh chose to ignore her. 'What about yourself there, Maureen? What do you fancy?'

'Hmm,' Maureen ran her eyes over the menu. 'I'm tempted by the fish of the day. Barracuda, isn't that what Jonas said?'

'It is.'

'Mummy, what should I have?' Noah asked. 'Nothing with yucky olives in it, please.'

'No, olives,' Roisin murmured, scanning the menu. 'What about a tomato pizza? You can't go wrong there?'

'Yay, pizza!'

Jonas waited patiently until, at last, everybody had made their minds up, and he went around the table in a clockwise direction, taking down their orders.

Maureen's attention returned to her wine once Jonas had hurried back inside the restaurant, and her hand rested on the stem, but she didn't pick it up just yet as she said to Bronagh, 'Do you know I'm beginning to think it's a conspiracy, like. One Irish restaurant owner said to another if we all start giving them a teeny-tiny drop of the wine with their dinner, they'll think the stuff costs an arm and a leg. That's why they're so miserly with it. Sure, it's like fine dining. You know, those places that serve up a meal where you need binoculars to locate what's on your plate, and you have to stop at the McDonald's on the way home. Just because it's expensive doesn't mean it's good. I'm all for good value like so,' she indicated her glass.

'I'm a woman who likes a deal, too, Maureen.'

Quinn was taking umbrage at the snippets of conversation he picked up on from across the way. He leaned over the table to correct his mother-in-law and O'Mara's receptionist on their opinion of Irish restaurateurs or at least him. 'Maureen, Bronagh, there's no mean little pours at my bistro, and none of our punters come away hungry so that you know.'

'I'll not argue with you there, Quinn. The girls have often rolled home after a night at Quinn's, and if you did, the teeny-tiny pours like they'd not be tripping up the stairs and falling into bed like so,' Maureen appeased.

'And, I've never had a stingy meal at Quinn's, that's for sure,' Bronagh added. 'You're very generous with the mashed potato, so.'

Satisfied it wasn't his restaurant they were casting in a skin-flinty light, Quinn returned to his pint. Then, as Aisling tugged at his arm, he twisted in his seat along with those on his side of the table to watch the unfolding show.

When they'd arrived, the first wisps of yellow had begun to mingle with the last vestiges of blue. Now, orange, pink and purple hues started streaking across the sky as the sun dropped further. Maureen reached for Donal's hand under the table. Her fingers entwined with his in a mutual understanding they were about to witness something magical. She lifted her wine glass with her other hand and held it to her nose, breathing in its top notes.

'What do you think, Bronagh? It's putting me in mind of a pine forest.'

'I'd agree with you there, Maureen. What do you think, Lenny?' She wafted it under her manfriend's nose.

'Pine-scented floor cleaner.'

'What about you, Donal?' Maureen waved her glass under his nose, hoping her live-in manfriend wasn't quite as much a heathen when it came to fine wines as Leonard Walsh was.

Donal gave it a sniff. 'Pine-scented Toilet Duck.'

Maureen and Bronagh shook their heads and, as Donal informed them it was traditional, called out 'Yammas!' as they clinked glasses in danger of sloshing the liquid onto the pristine white cloth.

'Bottoms up,' Maureen giggled, the heady effects of several champagne flutes not yet having worn off. She raised her glass to her lips, took a tentative sip, and shuddered. Then, braving another drink was pleasantly surprised by the burst of appley, peach beneath the astringent pine flavour in her mouth. She took a third sip, and it tasted even better this time and, putting her glass down on the table, declared it to be very good.

Bronagh smacked her lips together in satisfaction and nodded enthusiastically before announcing the wine to be fruity and piney with an underlying hint of Dettol. Then, following Maureen's lead, she took a second and third greedier swig.

'Jaysus wept. Would you listen to the pair of them carrying on like they're wine connoisseurs,' Moira said to Tom, who grinned amiably. He was happy to stick with the ale he'd ordered.

The sun dipped, so it was sitting on the horizon, a giant orb hovering between day and night. Then, finally, an orange tide rolled in, and no one spoke as they sat enjoying their drinks, watching the sun's last hurrah.

'Three, two, one,' some eejit counted down, and Maureen realised it was Pat and retracted her mental eejit comment as the sun ducked out of sight. There was a final intense pop of colour, and she held her breath without even realising she was doing so until she, and everyone else who'd been doing the same, sighed, and the sound was like wind whipping through the trees. *Pine trees*, she thought, finishing her drink as the colours faded into darkness.

'Bronagh, would it make better economic sense to order a carafe of the Retsina wine instead of a glass? Given we're both women who like a deal.'

'It would make perfect sense, Mo,' Bronagh replied, knocking back the remains of her drink and catching sight of Jonas, she waved out.

'Jonas, yoo-hoo! Could Maureen and myself have a carafe of the Retsina, please?'

Moira caught her sisters' eyes. 'They're on the carafe, the pair of them. This is not going to end well.'

Chapter Twenty

G eorgios held the dogeared postcard that had arrived in the mail a few months after Obelia left. Her address and telephone number were scribbled on the back of it. His daughter's way of telling him she wanted to hear from him. He'd put the card in the top drawer of the desk here in his pension's foyer. He pressed the phone hard to his ear, waiting for it to ring. His heart was pounding, and he loosened the buttons at the neck of his polo shirt. He would let it ring six times, and if no one answered, he'd hang up without leaving a message.

It was picked up on the fifth ring.

'*Yassou*,' a warm, rich voice so like her mána's answered.

His eyes misted. It was her. Obelia. He opened his mouth, but no sound came out.

'*Yassou*?' There was uncertainty in her voice now.

Speak, you fool, Georgios told himself, but all the things he wanted to say sat heavily on his heart, refusing to form coherent sentences.

There was the hiss of an annoyed sigh, and then the line went dead. Georgios tried to picture the apartment where she lived. Then, as the phone began to hurt his ear, he replaced it in its cradle. His face was hot with embarrassment at his behaviour. He was a man in his fifties, not a teenager.

'You're a fool, Georgios Kyrgios,' Ana's voice sounded in his head as though she was standing next to him.

'I know Ana, I know.' He ran his hands through his hair several times to shake off the melancholy. It did no good to allow it in for long because it didn't change anything; then, he made his way back to the kitchen.

The pension was silent without his boisterous Irish guests, and he thought Wendy would be wondering where he was, galvanising himself. The bottle of rosé they enjoyed a glass of over dinner was where he'd left it on the kitchen worktop, having put it down to make his impromptu phone call. Georgios picked it up with the loaf of crusty bread in a brown paper bag. Wendy had asked him to pick it up earlier, and tucking it under his arm, he strode purposefully to the front door.

There was no need to lock it behind him, and stepping outside he saw that it was his favourite time of the day when the world glowed briefly golden, and the possibilities seemed endless. He hoped his and Wendy's guests had found the sunset people travelled from around the globe to witness as spectacular as its reputation.

The scrawny ginger and white cat he'd taken to feeding was curled up territorially on the chair's cushion to the left of the door.

'Are you keeping guard?' he asked, pausing to tickle behind its ears.

The cat mewled its reply, and spying a deadhead on the potted geraniums, he plucked it off and tossed it into the planter. It was a good job the flowers were hardy, he mused, because the plants dotted about the pension had been Ana's domain. He could turn his hand to most things, but he'd not been blessed with green fingers.

'*Kalispera,*' the youngest son of the Castellanos family, who'd lived here in Karterados for as long as he had, called out as he kicked his football over to him.

'Kalisper.' Georgios kicked it back, and the boy continued to nudge the ball up the road as he walked the few short steps to Stanley's. The door was open, as he'd known it would be, and he stepped inside the foyer area where the photographs Wendy had taken and framed to hang on her walls were shadowed as the light outside began to fade. He sniffed the spiced, meaty aroma that filled the air appreciatively and pushed the door closed behind him, hazarding a guess Stifado was on tonight's menu. 'Yassou!' He called out before stepping inside the kitchen, not wanting to frighten his neighbour even though she was expecting him.

'Yassou. We're having Stifado.' Wendy was standing before the temperamental cooker, sprinkling parsley on the simmering stew.

Georgios mentally congratulated himself on guessing correctly.

She rubbed her hands together, and a few fresh green sprigs fell onto the meat, before turning to look at Georgios, taking note of the loaf he'd placed down on her stone countertop. 'Good, you didn't forget the bread. We'll need it to mop up the juices.'

'Or, and more importantly, in my opinion, the wine.' Georgios raised the bottle and received a smile in return. She had a nice smile. It lit up her whole face. Wendy was a woman whose smile always reached her eyes. 'It smells wonderful.'

'I hope you're hungry because there's plenty here.'

'You know me. I am always hungry.'

This time his reward was a laugh.

Georgios moved around the kitchen, sorely needing renovation, with familiar ease, uncorking the wine and sloshing it into the two glasses he retrieved from the Welsh Dresser. It was one of the few possessions Wendy had brought with her from England, saying it had belonged to her mother and was of great sentimental value. His gaze flicked over the crumbling, dense plaster walls, designed as such to keep the heat out. The stone countertop was small, and the cabinetry built into it and the sink, also stone, he knew had a spidering crack running through its deep basin. *How his neighbour churned out such delicious meals here was a mystery,* he thought not for the first time. He'd offered to help her modernise it in keeping with the rest of her pension, but Wendy said she loved the authenticity of her kitchen and was adamant it helped rather than hindered her culinary skills. He shook his head and set the wine on the table before fetching the placemats and cutlery. Then, as Wendy served the stew, he sawed into the bread.

He carried the breadboard to the table where two steaming bowls of the Stifado were waiting to be enjoyed. Wendy retrieved the butter, and then they sat at the table, clinking glasses and savouring that first sip of wine.

'Have you met Bronagh, who's staying with me?' Wendy asked, putting her glass down and picking up her fork.

Georgios nodded. 'With the black hair like Cleopatra.'

'That's her. She works as the receptionist at the guesthouse, Maureen, who is staying with you, used to run with her late husband. Her daughter Aisling, the sister with the glorious mane of red-gold hair, runs it now.'

Georgios dipped his head again, trying to follow along, recalling Maureen telling him some of this earlier.

'Well, the guesthouse was how Bronagh met Leonard.'

Georgios pictured the quietly spoken man with knee-high socks and sandals.

'He was a guest who used to come and stay annually at O'Mara's to visit his sister, who lives in Dublin. I didn't like to ask why he didn't just stay with her. And, then, there's Maureen and Donal. Maureen met him at a party where he was singing in a band.'

'Ah, yes. I've heard this story. The Kenny Rogers cover band.' He'd been amused by it and relayed how the couple had settled their grand-daughter by singing the Kenny Rogers, Dolly Parton duet, 'Islands in the Stream'.

Wendy clapped her hands together. 'How delightful!'

Georgios agreed it had been something to see.

'Do you know Bronagh told me Maureen was heartbroken when her husband died, but when she met Donal, she took on a new lease of life?'

Georgios murmured, 'Mmm' absently. It wasn't like Wendy to be so interested in the romantic lives of their guests, and he wondered what the point of her conversation was. But then, his mind drifted away from their Irish guests and back to his attempted phone call to Obelia.

Wendy's sigh was wistful. 'It's lovely hearing stories like that. It proves there are second chances for everyone.'

'Second chances for what?' Georgios tuned back into the tail end of what she'd been saying.

'You can be very dense at times, Georgios Kyrgios.' Wendy's tone spiked with annoyance. 'For finding love is what.'

Did Wendy want to find someone to see out the rest of her days with? The notion surprised him because he'd thought she was content here running her pension. The idea of her meeting a man to share her life with perturbed him because where would it leave him? The third wheel sat at the dinner table, that's where. He told himself off for thinking such self-centred thoughts. She had every right to seek a new relationship if she thought it would make her happy.

Wendy sighed and put her glass down. He could feel her eyes upon him as he toyed with his food. His appetite was uncharacteristically deserting him.

He was pushing one of the sweet pearl onions swimming in the aromatic gravy around his dish when Wendy put her fork down and said, 'Alright, Georgios. Come on. What's bothering you?'

'Nothing is bothering me. How could there be when I have a meal fit for the Gods in front of me?'

'Georgios, you've barely touched it.' Wendy picked up her glass and eyed him contemplatively. 'And you are a man who enjoys his food.'

'This is true.' He gave her a wry smile across the table.

'So tell me what's on your mind so we can enjoy dinner.' Wendy tucked her brown hair, shot through with silver, behind her ears and waited expectantly.

Georgios exhaled and put his fork down, sipping his rosé before confessing. 'I telephoned Obelia.'

A light glowed in Wendy's eyes, and Georgios watched as it went out when he told her he'd not spoken, having hung up on her. Then, finally, he shrugged, 'I couldn't find the words.'

'She's your daughter, Georgios,' Wendy said softly. 'All you need to tell her is that you love her. Three little words.'

'It's not that simple.' Georgios put his wine glass down with more force than was necessary. It was frustrating because deep down, he knew Wendy was right. It was that simple.

His flash or irritation didn't phase Wendy. 'She has a right to live her own life, Georgios. Our children are only on loan. They're not ours to keep.'

'Her life was here with me and her mána.' He knew he was being stubborn and, yes, even selfish, but still, he could not help himself. 'All that we built,' he flapped his hand in the vague direction of his pension, 'with Kyrgios's was for her, and she threw it in my face. You know this, Wendy.'

Wendy put her glass down, squaring up to him across the table. 'Her mother is gone, Georgios, and don't forget I knew Ana. Yes, she hoped Obelia would make her life here with you on the island, but that was because she was frightened of leaving you alone. But, this,' she threw her hands out in frustration, 'with you and Obelia, it is far from what she would have wanted. I think if Ana were here with us now, she'd recognise and accept Obelia has hopes and dreams of her own that are bigger than Santorini.'

The fight went out of Georgios, and his shoulders slumped. 'I know this in here,' he tapped his chest. 'But I don't know how to say it.'

'I could help you.'

Hope flared. 'You will talk to her?'

'No, Georgios. That's for you to do, but we can work out what you want to tell her together if you like.'

He nodded, his appetite slowly returning because he might have a chance of getting his daughter back after all.

Chapter Twenty-one

♥

T he inky sky was sparkling with stars, and the air was like a warm, friendly kiss as they strolled from the taverna where they'd enjoyed dinner, courtesy of Big Jim and Bea, down the streets of Oia. It was a little after 9.30 pm, and the touristy village was teeming with life. Maureen winced hearing someone, somewhere not too far away, murdering Kim Carnes, Betty Davis Eyes, in a karaoke bar. Next, they were off to a supper club holding a late, traditional Greek night show that Jonas had recommended they visit after dinner. The waiter had promised them the works: plate smashing, traditional music and song, and the all-important crowd-pleasing, Sirtaki dancing. Upon hearing this, Maureen and Bronagh, who were pink-cheeked, had insisted on draping their arms around Jonas's shoulders and doing a sort of can-can.

'Mammy, Bronagh, what do you think you're doing?' Aisling had asked.

'It's Mo-C and Bro-T to you,' Maureen informed her, giving an impressively high leg kick, 'The Zorba Greek dancing, of course.'

Aisling, Moira, Roisin and even Patrick all shook their heads.

'Kiera, don't look at your Nana there making a holy show of herself,' Moira sniffed, but it was too late. Kiera was giggling, thinking Nana and Bronagh were hysterical. That, or she'd slipped into the dangerous zone of being overtired.

Jonas had given them detailed instructions on navigating the labyrinth of lanes that would lead them to the club after much back-slapping between himself and Big Jim. Maureen had whispered in a voice fuzzy around the edges, to Donal that given the enthusiasm with which Jonas was thwacking the American man, he must have slipped him a sizeable tip. They'd all thanked Big Jim and Bea profusely for their generosity, expounding on what a lovely meal they'd had and then, as they left the taverna, their party suddenly shrank. Roisin, Aisling and Moira begged off, saying they'd babbies, children and husbands needing to be put to bed. It had tickled her to think she was stopping out later than her daughters these days. It tickled her further when they'd each told her to behave herself and not stop out late!

'They've no stamina these young wans, Bro-T,' Maureen had leaned in to inform Bronagh, who was staring up at the night sky as though seeing it for the first time.

Bobby-Jean, Sherry, Patrick and Cindy were chatting about all things wedding followed dutifully behind their self-appointed guides. At the same time, Donal and Leonard discussed the flakiness of the Baklava's filo pastry they'd enjoyed for dessert. Meanwhile, Maureen and Bronagh were lagging in last place, intent on not toppling over on the uneven paving.

'I had a word with Pat and Cindy to say I thought they might be better getting an early night, but Cindy said this last tri-tri,' Maureen couldn't get her mouth to form the word.

'I know the word you mean,' Bronagh said.

'Grand. She said these last few months of pregnancy have her feeling full of beans.' Maureen decided to leave out that her son's fiancée had also said she was finding it hard to keep her hands off Pat at the moment too. Her hormones were rampant, and she'd pinched his bottom to prove her point.

'She's certainly full of something. The belly on her.'

They lapsed into companionable silence until Maureen frowning, spoke up. 'Bro-T, what are we going to do about Georgios and Wendy?' She might not know much about Georgios, but she knew an eligible widower when she saw one. Bronagh had told her about Wendy having decided to start a new life in Santorini after her husband passed away. She'd only caught a glimpse of Georgios's neighbour as she waved them off on their mule riding expedition earlier but had thought her attractive, and she'd looked to be a similar age to Georgios. A match made in heaven, in her opinion.

'I don't know Mo-C, but it's a crying shame them both being on their own.'

'Tis a crying shame,' Maureen agreed, glad Bronagh had her arm as she rocked in her heels like a sunflower swaying in the breeze.

'I say we play it by ear. Sure, we have a good few days left to come up with something to make them realise they're made for each other.'

'We have. A good few days.' Maureen echoed, nearly walking into Donal as he abruptly stopped. Bronagh doing the same thanks to Big Jim's sudden stop. He was eyeing the name of the street displayed on a blue plaque with white lettering on the side of a shop.

'This is the street down here, y'all!' he drawled victoriously a second later.

'We knew you'd find it, Daddy!' Sherry exclaimed, and Maureen knew if Moira were here, she'd be making noises about fecky brown-nosers. *Cindy's sister was probably hoping Daddy would foot the bill for the drinks while they watched the show, too*, she thought.

'You've still got it, my Big Man,' Bea said in a husky voice that saw Bronagh and Maureen look at one another, alarmed. There was a time and a place for the husky voice, and it wasn't on a crowded street with your new family in Santorini. Bea looked over her shoulder at them all. 'What this beefcake man of mine can do with a compass has to be seen to be believed.'

'We'll take your word on that, Bea,' Bobby-Jean replied quickly, swinging back toward the rest of the group and mouthing, 'TMI.'

They veered off to the right, winding their way down the fairy light-lit lane, so narrow it was single file only. Music pulsated around them, adding to the festive vibe.

'Calimari,' Maureen sang to fellow revellers squeezing past in the opposite direction.

'It's *Kalispera*, Mo,' Donal piped up.

'That's what I said, Donal,' Maureen said, thinking she'd be sure to remind Donal to get his ears checked when they got home.

They all came to a standstill once more and squinting around the others to see what was happening, Maureen realised they were at the end of a long line of people. Word filtered down to her and Bronagh that this was the queue to get into the club. Jonas had forgotten to mention how popular it was.

'Jaysus wept. I can't be queuing now.' Bronagh said, alarmed. 'I need to spend a penny. It's the Retsina. It's not going to wait for anybody.'

'Bro-T can't be waiting long. She needs to spend a penny.' Maureen cupped her hands on either side of her mouth to call up the line.

'Leave it with me,' Cindy called back.

'Don't be making me laugh now,' Bronagh warned Maureen, crossing her legs as a precaution.

Cindy appeared a second later, 'Come on, Mom, Bronagh, we're in.' She gestured for them to follow her and the others past the queuing minions.

'What did you say?' Maureen asked as the burly fellow in the suit held the door open for them. She avoided eye contact with the disgruntled crowd still waiting to enter the club.

'I passed myself and Pat off as David Hasselhoff and a pregnant Pamela Anderson. I told the bouncer we were here to film Baywatch Santorini the Second Generation, and so far as he's concerned, you're all extras.'

'That was smart thinking, Cindy, and Pat does have a look of yer man David now you mention it.'

'Well, I'll not be doing the jog down the beach until I've been to the ladies, like,' Bronagh said, hobbling into the smoky club knock-kneed.

The drinks were flowing and the laughter loud as people rubbed shoulders in the crowded club while a lucky few had commandeered the tables centred around a sunken stage area in the middle of the deceptively large space. In the middle of the stage, a young man in a white shirt, black pants and black cap was spotlighted as he plucked the strings of a Bouzouki expertly and sang mournfully.

Bronagh left them to it as she elbowed her way through to the powder room, but the power of celebrity name-dropping meant those she left behind didn't have to wait long to be seated. Word had spread amongst the staff, and they were ushered over to two tables pushed together at the edge of the stage area, and as they all sat down, there was mutual agreement amongst them all that they'd have a bird's eye view of the evening's promised performance.

Big Jim offered Cuban cigars around, and Donal and Leonard said they didn't mind if they did. Maureen hadn't seen Donal smoke a cigar before, and once he'd stopped coughing, he seemed to find it very relaxing. Clouds of pungent smoke formed a haze above their heads.

The club offered table service, and as there was no sign of Bronagh, Maureen took it upon herself to order another Retsina carafe to share.

It was going down a treat, so it was, she thought as Donal asked her if she were sure she wouldn't rather have a nice glass of water.

'Water? Sure, I can get that at home. What would I want with the H2O?' Maureen shook her head in disgust. It wasn't like Donal to be such an eejit. She saw Bronagh looking about the place and waved out. 'Bro-T, c'mere to me now, you good woman you. Donal's after suggesting I have water.'

'Sure, Donal, what would she want with water? Can't she drink that any old time?' Bronagh said, sitting down next to Maureen. She spied Leonard chuffing away on his plump cigar. 'There's something about a man and a cigar that's very attractive.'

Maureen was inclined to agree. But, mind you, two carafes of Retsina and yer little weasley man with the bad sunburn and the comb-over sitting two tables away was beginning to look like a candidate for the Chippendales.

Bobby-Jean's blonde curls shimmered despite the dim lighting, and Maureen waved over, 'Are you enjoying the craic, Bo-J?'

Bobby-Jean's mascara-heavy eyes widened as she leaned over Sherry to ask, 'Mo-C, did you ask me if I have a crack?'

Bronagh and Maureen looked at one another. What was she on about? 'No. I asked you if you were enjoying the craic, like.'

Bobby-Jean looked none the wiser.

'They didn't strike me as the sort to be into drugs,' Sherry, sipping a pink cocktail, drawled in Bobby-Jean's ear.

Patrick, who'd been eyeing the cloud of smoke over their heads with disapproval, stepped in to explain the meaning behind craic, but Maureen and Bronagh were more interested in pouring their carafe that had just arrived. The rest of the drinks were delivered and began piling up on the table, with a few token bowls of olives and a container of toothpicks. Although what they were supposed to do to help soak up the alcohol was anybody's guess, Donal told Leonard. The two men exhaled their plumes of smoke and looked to their lady loves sloshing wine into their glasses with a shake of their heads.

Patrick announced he and Cindy had decided the second-hand smoke was too much and, saying goodnight, left them to it.

'We've got to be ready for the show, Bro-T,' Maureen said, putting the carafe back on the table.

'Show ready,' Bronagh agreed, lifting her full glass to her lips.

'What's that instrument your mournful man's after playing? Yer fella at the restaurant was strumming the same thing.'

'Is it a banjo?' Bronagh squinted at the stage.

Donal, catching wind of their conversation, supplied them with the answer. 'It's called a Bouzouki.'

'He's playing his Bouzouki,' Maureen said, then sounded the word again. 'Bouzouki.'

She and Bronagh found this hilarious. Donal failed to see what the joke was.

'Ooh, look Bro-T, something's happening, yer man there's off the stool.' Maureen pointed to where the mournful singing man dragged his stool away from the spotlight. A smattering of applause sounded around the stuffy club, although whether it was because the mournful singing was over or to show appreciation for his musical talent Maureen was uncertain. He'd no sooner disappeared when he reappeared once more with his Bouzouki still in hand, only this time he was flanked by a man with a sort-a violin and another with a teeny-tiny guitar.

'The violin-looking yoke is a Cretan Lyra, and the ukelele wan is a Baglamas,' Donal jumped in, and Maureen puffed up proudly.

'He's very knowledgeable about all things Greek, is Donal,' she said to Bronagh.

'My Lennie's a man of the world himself,' Bronagh said. 'And, sure, look it, he can blow the smoke rings.'

They both looked to where Leonard was sending perfect bluish-grey rings toward the ceiling. 'Can you do the smoke rings, Donal?' Maureen asked hopefully.

'No.'

The musicians took their place down the back of the stage area, and after much applause and cries of '*Opa*', three women came prancing in. They were dressed in simple white cotton dresses with draping sleeves, silky powder blue waistcoats and matching aprons. Three men skipped in to join them, clad in white shirts, black coats with red trim and red silk sashes worn over baggy black pants. On their heads, they wore tasselled caps.

'Don't they look smart?' Maureen said.

'They do Mo-C. Will your Pat be wearing something similar on the day?

'I don't know, Bro-T. You know Pat, he always likes to look the part. I hope he doesn't wear a cap, though. It would make his head look too small for his body.'

The dancers joined hands and began to perform their synchronised steps expertly. *The music was infectious, and you couldn't help but clap along*, Maureen thought, doing just that. She itched to join them down on the stage and have a go herself. Bronagh's toes were tapping impatiently, too, and it wasn't long before the performers urged the clubs' patrons to do just that. Maureen and Bronagh shot out of their seats and down onto the stage, throwing their arms over the shoulders of the dancers and clicking their fingers in the appropriate places to the piece of music made famous by the film 'Zorba the Greek'. Other patrons filed down to join them, and soon a large circle had formed as the dancers did their best to get them to follow suit with the steps to the slow tempo.

Maureen was having the time of her life, occasionally shouting '*Opa*' in between telling the man with the baggy pants she'd hooked onto that she was Irish, which meant the fancy footwork was in her blood. She put the right leg in and the left foot out at the proper times until, gradually, the music picked up the pace, and suddenly her little arms and legs were going everywhere. A sunflower in a cyclone. She was beginning to feel hot and slightly dizzy at the speed of it all, and as the song finally concluded, she sent up a silent prayer of thanks before staggering back to her seat.

Donal told her she'd done well and was a natural at the Greek dancing as she cast about for her wine glass. It had disappeared, as had the carafe. In its place was a tray of shot glasses containing a clear liquid. Maureen picked one up and sniffed at it. It smelled like aniseed.

'Big Jim thought we were due a round of Ouzos,' Donal explained.

'That's good of him. He's a good man is Big Jim, and I'm verra verra thirsty from all that dancing.'

'Mo, I think—'

He was too late because Maureen had knocked back the sweet, licoricey liquid. She hiccupped and put the empty glass down as Bronagh flopped down alongside her.

'I'm verra, verra thirsty. What's those?'

'Sure, it's lolly water,' Maureen passed her a glass.

Their heads were lolling by the time the plate smashing began in earnest.

Chapter Twenty-two

'Tell my children I love them, Donal,' Maureen whimpered, squinting as the room filled with sunlight because she was surely on her last legs.

Donal was standing by the window, enthusiastically pulling the curtains open.

She pulled the sheet over her head and burrowed in bed, intending to sleep the day away.

'C'mon with you now, Mo. You'll live. It's time to get up. You and Bronagh are after arranging to meet Bobby-Jean in Oia to go shopping this morning, and you can't be letting either of them down.'

Maureen groaned from the depths of her pit like a bear coming out of hibernation because she knew he was right. She didn't let people down. It wasn't in her DNA to do so. She was, and always had been, a people pleaser. Besides, if she were to wallow here all day, the girls wouldn't give her a minute's peace. They'd all be barging in to sing The 'Soldier On' song she used to sing to them when they were feigning illness to get out of something or other they didn't want to be doing at school.

'And I'll not be telling you I told you so. So, you don't have to be worrying about that.'

'Told me what?' Maureen popped her head out from under the sheet, and it took a minute for her brain to catch up.

'To drink the water instead of another round of that Retsina, and as for the shots of Ouzo, well, you and Bronagh were knocking them back like it was lemonade, so you were.'

'Ah no, don't remind me, Donal!' Maureen tossed the sheet off the bed, hauling herself upright and stampeded into the bathroom as the memory of paint stripper and liquorice-laced alcohol sprang up in her throat.

When she emerged, having showered, which had made her feel a little better, Donal was standing at the ready armed with paracetamol and water.

'Get that down yer. Sure, a cup of coffee with something to eat, and you'll be good as new.'

Maureen wished she shared his conviction.

***

A short while later, she was slowly working through the strong coffee Georgios had put down in front of her. It was bitter and not to her taste, but he'd assured her the thick brew would enable her to rejoin the human race. She'd take his word for it. She'd take anything to ease the drilling behind her eyeballs right now. A piece of toast lay untouched on the plate in front of her, but she had managed to get one slice down her. As someone stirred their tea or coffee, she winced. Sounds were magnified this morning, with each scrape of a knife or clink of a spoon only intensifying the pounding in her head. And, she loved Donal; she really did, but she wished he'd not chosen to enjoy a hardboiled egg this morning because the smell of it was turning her tummy.

Maureen didn't even have the energy to glare at Moira, who kept saying things like, 'Mammy, would you like a greasy fry up?' Instead, she took another sip of the coffee and reassessed her physicality. Upon entering the dining room twenty minutes earlier, she felt marginally better than she had. The paracetamol had kicked in, and Georgios was right. The coffee was helping with the toast, putting a lining on her stomach. She would live, after all. The thought of spending a morning in Bronagh's company perked her up further because, as the saying went, 'Misery loved company', and her friend was likely to be feeling just as rough. *Bronagh*. Maureen sounded her name out in her head, deciding the novelty of the abbreviated nicknames had worn off in the cold, well, it was actually rather warm, light of day.

Maureen heard a click but didn't bother to look over. 'Moira, if you take one more photograph of me with that camera, I'll not be responsible for my actions.'

'But Mammy, it's for your own good. The next time you reach for the wine, I'll show you the Green Teletubby photographs, and you'll think twice.'

Maureen was very tempted to do a rude finger sign, but Kiera was nodding along with what her mammy was saying like a wise old lady, and she'd not be teaching her any bad habits.

'Poor you, Mammy,' Roisin said, instantly elevating herself to favourite daughter status. 'But I don't know what possessed you and Bronagh to behave like you were twenty-year-olds out on the lash, like.' She shook her head with the same sort of disgust Maureen used to reserve for her when inspecting her teenage bedroom.

Roisin was instantly demoted.

'Do you think you're able for some cereal Mo?' Donal asked, concern etched on his face and egg in his beard.

'No, you're grand, thanks, Donal.' *She was a lucky woman*, she thought, even if the hardboiled egg wasn't helping her delicate disposition. She remembered the smoke rings. *A man couldn't be good at everything now*, she told herself. 'What will you do with yourself this morning, Donal?'

'I think a lazy morning by the pool is in order.'

'Are you not off for a massage then, Donal?' Moira said with pretended innocence.

'I'll not tell you again, Moira.' Maureen shot feebly across at her daughter. Oh, what she wouldn't give to hide behind her sunglasses and stretch out on a sun lounger for the foreseeable future. She'd committed, though, and it was very kind of Bobby-Jean to offer to take her and Bronagh shopping. It wasn't every day you had a stylist at your disposal. They'd have to push through the pain, like when you were in the labour, and make the most of it. Donal was still speaking, she realised.

'And, I thought this afternoon we might check out the Red Beach.'

'That's not the beach where Patrick and Cindy are going to say their vows is it?'

'No, that's Kamari Beach. It's a black sand beach, and we're going there tomorrow morning for a look-see. The Red Beach has red sand. It's a geological wonder.'

What was wrong with your bog-standard golden sands? Maureen grumped silently as she tuned him out. Finally, when he'd finished spouting about geological rock formations and volcanic eruptions, she gave a weak, 'Grand.' Then draining the dregs in her cup, pushed back her chair. 'I'd best be heading next door to see if Bronagh's ready.'

'I'll come with you,' Donal said, wiping his mouth with a napkin and mercifully dislodging the bit of yolk from his beard.

'Maureen, are you feeling better?' Georgios asked, touting a fresh pot of coffee as he exited the kitchen. Amusement mingled with concern seeing his pasty-faced, bloodshot-eyed guest dragging her feet toward the front entrance. He made a tutting sound. 'The Retsina.'

'And Ouzo,' Donal added.

'Yes, alright, Donal. I don't need reminding.'

'Fun at the time but so ferocious the morning after.'

'They should come with a warning,' Maureen muttered, flicking her sunglasses down in preparation for the glare outside.

'You're off exploring?'

'Shopping. I'm going next door to see if Bronagh's ready.'

'Ah, and was your friend Bronagh as enthused with our Retsina and Ouzo?'

The very words should be banned, Maureen thought. *They were bad words, and she never wanted to hear them spoken of again.* 'She was.'

'Well, she'll be in good hands with Wendy. I taught her how to make the Greek coffee, too.'

Maureen's eyes narrowed behind her sunglasses. At the mention of his neighbour, she'd seen the light spark in his eyes that were the same colour as the coffee he was so proud of. There was no time to dwell on it further, though, because Donal held the door open for her, and Georgios was padding off toward the dining room.

'Enjoy your shopping, Mo.' Donal kissed her cheek.

'And, you enjoy your pool time.' Maureen gave a fluttery wave as he closed the door and, setting forth, nearly tripped over the scrawny ginger cat with tufts of white fur who'd mooched over to see if she'd anything to offer. She didn't want to risk bending down to pet the stray cat, what with her poor head, but did pause to explain she wasn't feeling one hundred per cent this morning and if he'd like to venture around the back, he'd find any number of people willing to pat and fuss him. Then, hoping he didn't have the worms or fleas, she took the few short steps to Stanley's.

Chapter

Twenty-three

B ronagh was perched on the cane-backed sofa. Her face, or at
least what Maureen could see of it, given she'd donned an enormous pair of black sunglasses, was erring toward a shade of lime.
But, before Maureen could commiserate with her, Wendy made a
jack-in-the-box-like appearance from behind the reception desk.

'Good morning there. It's Maureen, isn't it? We've not been properly introduced. I'm Wendy.'

Maureen thought it should be illegal to be that perky of a morning,
although it was a little infectious, and she'd a lovely, warm way about
her. 'It is, and it's a pleasure to make your acquaintance, Wendy.'

A groaning sounded from the sofa, echoing about the tiled space,
and both women looked to its source.

'Never again, Maureen.'

'Never again,' Maureen agreed, pleased Bronagh had dropped the
Mo-C business.

'Tis the life of the teetotaller for us both from here on in.'

'The life of the teetotaller,' Maureen agreed.

Wendy laughed. 'I have to tell you ladies; it's not the first time I've heard that from guests who've overindulged on some of Greece's delights.'

At least they weren't the first eejits to hit the Retsina and Ouzo like they were living their best life, Maureen thought, looking about. 'Where's Leonard?'

'He's enjoying a leisurely breakfast with Aisling, Quinn and the babbies. The man's a saint. A saint, I tell you, Maureen. I woke to a glass of water and two paracetamols. Then he ran the shower for me. And Wendy's an angel because she made me the coffee that you could stand a spoon up in, and I've eaten a slice of toast, although I had to make that myself.'

Maureen remembered the smoke rings and hastily dropped in, 'Well, Bronagh, I must tell you Donal's up there with Saint Patrick himself. Sure, he was after doing the same for me this morning, and he made me the toast.'

Bronagh opened her mouth to reply but ran out of steam.

'You'll be alright, Bronagh. Mark my words that cup of coffee I made you will sort you out, and in another five minutes, when the caffeine hits your bloodstream, you'll be back doing the Zorba dance.'

'Georgios said more or less the same to me this morning. He swears by the Greek coffee for getting rid of the banging head.'

'He taught me how to make proper Greek coffee.' Wendy smiled, and her eyes softened.

Somewhere through her hazy hungover fug, Maureen remembered the conversation she'd shared with Bronagh last night about their hosts, Georgios and Wendy. The tempering of Wendy's eyes as she said Georgios's name just now had set off a ding, ding, dinging, which was a welcome respite from the bang, bang, banging in her head. So, she quickly deduced, Wendy had feelings for Georgios, and Georgios, she suspected, wasn't aware of it yet, but he had feelings for Wendy. *Well, now, that would have to change*, she thought.

An impatient honking sounded.

'That will be your taxi, ladies. Enjoy your morning shopping.'

'Why don't you join us, Wendy?' The words tumbled out of Maureen's mouth.

Wendy looked surprised. 'Oh. Thank you for the invitation, but I've things to see to here.'

'Sure, what things?' Maureen warmed to her theme with a dismissive flap of her arm. 'The clearing of tables, dishwashing and bedmaking?'

'Yes. Those things.'

'They don't do themselves, do they?'

'No, they don't.'

'When did you last have a morning to yourself?'

'It's the nature of the business, Maureen.'

'I know I ran a guesthouse myself for years, but my daughter, Aisling eating her breakfast in there,' she gestured vaguely, unsure where the dining room was, 'she's in charge now and can turn her hand to anything you need doing.'

Maureen was brightening up as her plan formed while Bronagh looked on bewilderedly. 'And I'm offering you my daughter's services so you can have a well-deserved break and come and enjoy yourself with me and Bronagh. You'll love Bobby-Jean. She's a stylist to the stars, so we're in for a treat.'

Wendy was perplexed, and Maureen reading correctly that she couldn't tell whether she was joking, told her to tell the taxi man to hold his horses as he sat on his horn again, tagging on, 'I'm off to have a word with Aisling.'

'But you can't ask her to do the housework. She's a paying guest,' Wendy protested.

'Watch her,' Bronagh muttered, pointing Maureen in the right direction.

***

'Jaysus Mam,' Aisling said, the spoonful of cereal she was holding halfway to her mouth, 'you're the same colour as Bronagh.'

'Would you like me to whip up my hangover cure, Maureen?' Quinn offered chirpily.

'Does it involve raw eggs?'

'It does.'

Maureen swallowed hard. 'Then no, thank you. Good morning to you, Leonard.'

'Good morning, Maureen. It was a good night we were after having.'

'Better for some than others by the looks of things,' Aisling said.

'Aisling, that's not helpful, and my visit's not social because I've got a favour to ask of you.' Maureen explained she wanted to whisk Wendy into Oia with her and Bronagh to join Bobby-Jean, who would give them wardrobe tips in some of its exclusive boutiques.'

'But why?'

'So she can wow Georgios when they have dinner.'

'What dinner? Jaysus Mammy. You're like the cryptic crossword, so you are. Would you explain what you've in mind instead of dropping little clues?'

You'd think it was Aisling who'd been on the lash last night, given her tetchiness, Maureen thought. 'The dinner Quinn's going to cook for them.'

'Have I missed something.' Quinn frowned.

She was dealing with simpletons, Maureen thought, spelling it out. 'They're both widowed, and they've eyes for each other. They need a nudge to see that they're made for one another. And, I thought Bobby-Jean could help Wendy find the perfect dress for a romantic dinner with Georgios.'

'That neither of them knows anything about?'

'Exactly. Now you're cooking with gas.'

'That's a grand plan, Mammy.' Aisling was a born romantic and a sucker for a Cinderella story. 'Sure, I can make the rooms up, and Quinn can clear up here and do the dishes.'

'I'll dry,' Leonard volunteered.

'Tell her we'll have the place sorted in no time,' Aisling said.

Satisfied, Maureen went to kiss Aoife and Connor, but Aisling held her hand up. 'No, Mammy, don't be kissing the babbies with your boozy breath.'

Maureen left them to it and hustled back to reception. 'You're officially relieved of your duties, Wendy.'

'I've no excuse then, have I?' Wendy shook her head, finding herself swept along with the plans of the little Irish woman staying at Georgios's.

***

Unimpressed with waiting so long, the taxi driver succeeded in finding every pothole between Karterados and Oia. The jarring ride didn't do much for Maureen and Bronagh's dodgy hip flexors which were playing up thanks to the previous evening's high leg kicks, but the fact he'd his window wound right down meant they were blasted by fresh air, which did see off the last traces of their hangovers. Maureen recalled having arranged to meet Bobby-Jean outside Patrick and Cindy's resort at some point last night, but they'd no intention of intruding on the lovebirds this morning. Besides, Maureen had had enough aggravation from her daughters about her bad behaviour the night before. She wouldn't allow Patrick to put his ten penny's worth in. So it was they were loitering on the street outside Azure Waters, enjoying an autumnal, blue-skied Santorini morning as the sun gently warmed their skin.

Wendy told them a little about her background and how she'd come to buy a pension on Santorini while they waited, and Maureen found herself relating to the English woman's story. She'd done the same and packed up her life as she'd known it after Brian's passing. Dublin to Howth was hardly on the same scale as Yorkshire to Santorini, but it was still a big change. Like Wendy, she'd had no say in her husband being taken from her far too early, and it had left her bereft and feeling powerless, until one day she'd realised she did have control over what she chose to do next and that had been to forge a new and different path for herself.

Bronagh scanned the busy lane for Bobby-Jean, but there was no sign of her. 'Are you sure we said ten, Maureen?'

'I'm sure.' Maureen scoured the faces in the crowds and saw a rangy fellow waving out. He'd put on one of those porkpie hats and had teamed it with a blue shirt, and cream slacks. She dropped her sunglasses down to her nose for a better look, thinking him handsome if you liked the Hugh Grant with the foppish hair falling into his eyes type. *He couldn't be waving at them, though*, she thought, glancing back over her shoulder to see if he was trying to catch the attention of someone behind them, but nobody else was loitering nearby.

'Mo-C, Bro-T!' The man called out as he drew nearer.

Bronagh and Maureen looked at one another. Only one person would call them that, and they obviously still needed to get the memo about dropping the Mo-C Bro-T bit.

'Surely not.'

'It can't be.'

'It is,' Bobby-Jean grinned, stepping from the sea of people to join the three waiting women. 'It's me.'

Chapter

Twenty-four

'Bobby-Jean!' Maureen and Bronagh were stupefied by the transformation of their friend.

'The one and the same. I felt like a change yesterday, and today I'm back to being plain old Bobby-Gene with a G. G.E.N.E..' He spelt it out and then pulled a sad face. 'Bo-G doesn't have quite the same ring to it, does it?'

Wendy, tucking her hair behind her ears, laughed in confusion, then held her hand out. 'I thought you were a woman, sorry. I must have got my wires crossed. I'm Wendy, by the way. I run Stanley's Pension where Bronagh's staying, and I apologise for gate-crashing your outing like this, but Maureen and Bronagh can be very persuasive, and they insisted I tag along.'

'You're very welcome to join us, and your wires are very straight, Wendy. It is confusing because I was a woman yesterday, which is why Maureen and Bronagh's mouths are hanging open.' Bobby-Gene's eyes glimmered with amusement as he shook Wendy's hand. 'It's a pleasure to meet you.'

Maureen shut her mouth. 'Bobby-Gene's a cross-dresser,' she told Wendy, lowering her voice, 'And we don't say transvestite these days.'

'Oh. Right. Got it.' Now it was Wendy's eyes that were twinkling.

'Which means he, er...,' Bronagh's addled brain wasn't able for an explanation.

'He. You're on the right track, Bronagh. Wendy, the simplest way to put it is I'm a man who enjoys dressing in women's clothes when the mood takes me.'

'And tis very unfair because he looks very well either way,' Maureen supplied. 'And to clarify, you like women, not men, don't you Bobby-Gene?' She needed clarification herself.

'You've got it, Mo-C. I adore women.'

All three women sucked their tummies in subconsciously. Meanwhile, Wendy was flicking between Maureen and Bobby-Gene, trying to keep up.

'Do you think we could drop the Mo-C today, Bobby-Gene? Because it's giving me flashbacks to last night,' Maureen asked.

'And the Bro-T,' Bronagh was quick to add.

'No more Bo-J?'

'No more Bo-J,' the two Irish women confirmed.

'Or Bo-G?'

'Or Bo-G.'

'I take it you were suffering for your sins this morning, ladies?' Bobby-Gene took off his hat and pushed his hand through his hair before putting it back on.

'We were, weren't we, Bronagh?'

Bronagh nodded confirmation. 'Which is why we're teetotallers from this day forth.'

'Now, that is a shame because the concierge at the hotel where Sherry, Bea, Big Jim and I are staying recommended a fabulous winery for lunch that offered wine tastings and platters to enjoy while admiring a view to die for. It would be the perfect way to round off our morning shopping.'

'Well, now, there's always the hair of the dog, Maureen.'

'And visiting a winery is listed on the top ten things to do on Santorini, Bronagh,' Maureen added, then turning back to Bobby-Gene, asked, 'What is it the others have planned for the day?'

'Big Jim and Bea are relaxing at the resort this morning, and they were talking about taking a tour of the island's Venetian castles in the afternoon. Sherry will keep the girls on their toes with the wedding rehearsal and Patrick will probably chill by the pool.'

Maureen digested this while Wendy spoke up. 'Maureen and Bronagh told me you're a Los Angeles stylist, Bobby-Gene?' Wendy said as they began to head up the lane.

'I am, and I'm a celebrant. I love what I do.'

'Bobby-Gene's officiating at my son Patrick's wedding, Wendy.'

'Oh, lovely.'

'Bobby-Gene, do you know where the mood will take you to marry Pat and Cindy?' Maureen enquired. 'Not that I mind either way. I like to be in the know, is all.'

'I think Bobby-Jean's had enough island time, Maureen.'

'Grand.' Although Maureen was a little disappointed because she'd grown fond of Bobby-Jean. Still and all, she was sure she'd be equally fond of yer man here in no time, too. A thought occurred to her, and she was surprised it hadn't popped up before now, but her mind had been full of Pat and Cindy's wedding. 'Listen to me now, Bobby-Gene. You don't know my late husband's brother, Cormac O'Mara, now. He's a fashion designer, a well-known one at that over there in Los Angeles.'

Bobby-Gene grinned. 'Patrick introduced us. His shop's a favourite with my clientele.'

Maureen was pleased. She was very proud of Cormac. 'I haven't had a chance to speak to him in a while, and I'm hoping we're still on speaking terms when he finds out he wasn't invited to Pat's wedding.' Her frown was ferocious. 'My son and Cindy don't understand that weddings aren't just about the bride and groom. They're about the family too; when you're Irish, that means the extended family.' She sighed weightily. 'I suppose I can count my blessings the family re-union we were after having has been and gone because if that lot had caught wind there was to be a wedding in the family and they weren't invited, I'd have been given the silent treatment for sure.'

'It was short notice Maureen for obvious reasons. Can you imagine the logistics of trying to organise a big do in the time frame they had?' Bobby-Gene said. 'People will understand.'

Maureen wasn't so sure, but she could do nothing about it.

'It's nice keeping it small and intimate, like,' Bronagh piped up, although if she'd not been included in the immediate family equation, her nose would have been properly out of joint.

'My son had an enormous wedding,' Wendy said. 'It cost him and his wife an absolute fortune, and the stress of organising it all and trying to keep both sides of the family happy nearly saw them call the whole thing off. All the hoo-ha sucked a lot of the joy from it for them. I think it's easy to lose sight of what getting married is supposed to be about when things get too big.'

Maureen mulled this over thoughtfully. 'I can see your point, right enough, Wendy, and I suppose by the time the O'Maras gather en masse like so again, they'll have forgotten all about the wedding snub.'

'Exactly,' Bronagh said, clapping her hands. 'C'mon now. We can't stand chatting all morning. We've shopping to be getting on with. Is there somewhere you've got in mind to take us this morning, Bobby-Gene?' Bronagh asked, linking her arm through Wendy's, ready for the off.

'I scoped out a silk shop on Main Street, not far from here, yesterday. It had some beautiful pieces. So that's going to be our first port of call.'

'Silk,' Maureen murmured. 'Sounds expensive.'

'Ladies, I firmly believe that splurging on quality accessories like a silk scarf is a worthy investment because it will instantly elevate any outfit to the next level. In addition, it makes a statement about who you are.'

'Well, I'm not a nylon lady, that's for sure,' Bronagh said. 'Lead the way, Bobby-Gene.'

Maureen linked her arm through Bobby-Gene's, and they headed up the lane, taking a right hairpin turn a little further up. It was a slow journey because there was so much to ooh and aah over along the way. The colours on display inside and outside the hole-in-the-wall shops, be it trinkets or artisan crafts, were joyous, and the vibe on the twisty, stone-cobbled streets was lively and energetic.

'Here we are,' Bobby-Gene said, stopping short of the base of the stone steps ahead of them to indicate an open doorway on their right. Above the yawning entrance was a blue and mustard handwritten sign proclaiming they'd found The Silk Shop. 'It used to be a bakery, apparently,' Bobby-Gene said before examining the vibrant plain and patterned pashminas, and scarfs knotted over the outside rail with a practised eye. Bronagh and Wendy pushed past him, eager to poke around inside, and Maureen, seeing the coast was finally clear, seized the moment. It was the first opportunity she'd had to divulge the plan she'd in mind for Wendy's transformation. 'Bobby-Gene, listen up because I'm only going to say this once.'

'Maureen, were you a fan of 'Get Smart' by chance?'

'There's no time for chit-chat,' Maureen admonished, launching into how Wendy was widowed like Georgios, who owned the pension next door to hers where she was staying with Donal, Moira, Rosi and co. 'Wendy's mad about him, and I think he feels the same way, only he will need to be nudged along. So, what we're thinking is this.' She finished by giving him his mission should he choose to accept it. To find an outfit that would ensure the blinkers fell off Georgios's eyes, and he saw her not as his neighbour but as the woman he was in love with.

Bobby-Gene's eyes were alight with excitement. 'Maureen, I accept the mission. It's right up my alley.'

***

A half an hour or so later, under the direction of a fellow tourist who'd raved about a boutique she'd stumbled across called Sunset, they reluctantly left The Silk Shop. The three women each were toting a bag containing their extravagant silken purchase.

Maureen and Bronagh had opted for an eye-catching scarf on top of which Maureen had forked out for one in teal, purple, gold and silver for each of her girls, Cindy included then, worrying Sherry would feel left out, she bought her one in coral. She and Bronagh had both been smitten with the hot pink and the turquoise scarfs Bobby-Gene had picked out, and there'd been a debate over who'd be knotting what jauntily. In the end, Bobby-Gene settled matters by telling them they could always swap with another but that the pink colour brought out a glow in Maureen's cheeks, and the turquoise gave Bronagh an exotic air.

The word 'exotic' sealed the deal for Bronagh, who whipped the turquoise scarf off Maureen and held it up over the lower half of her face like a Saudi Arabian princess. Then, with a flutter of her eyelashes, she announced she'd always wanted to be exotic as she demonstrated a belly dance that had them all in stitches. As for Wendy, she'd said she really shouldn't, in the way you did when you knew you were going to, and was now the proud owner of an emerald green silk pashmina. Little did she know as they set off for their next destination, her new friends were all in cahoots to find the perfect dress for her to drape it over.

Sunset Boutique Jewellery and Clothing was easy to find, but they'd have been sure to miss it if not for the woman in the silk shop's recommendation. Bobby-Gene herded them inside and, within minutes, had picked out three beautifully simple dresses and pushed a protesting Wendy toward the fitting room.

'I can't afford any of these.'

'You can't not afford one of these,' Bobby-Gene shot back as Wendy stepped inside the changing cubicle, and he pulled the curtain across.

The woman behind the counter was conversing deeply with a customer about the merits of cotton. Maureen, like Pooh Bear to a pot of honey, had been drawn to the jewellery cabinet and was admiring the eclectic range of handcrafted sparkly things while Bronagh was drooling over a red and white polka-dot halter neck dress that saw Bobby-Gene shake his head as he turned his attention toward her. He crossed the shop floor swiftly and began flicking through the racks of predominantly linen and cotton clothes at breakneck speed before producing a yellow linen shift dress. Maureen thought you could tell he'd done this sort of thing hundreds of times before, admiring his assertiveness.

'Bronagh, what about this?'

'It's a yellow potato sack. I like a bit of shape in my clothes and the polka dots.'

'It's linen, and the shift is a flattering shape and length with the added bonus of being comfortable. This yellow shade, with its mustard hints, will contrast beautifully with your turquoise scarf. You should try it on.'

Bronagh's expression was mutinous as she looked from the dress Bobby-Gene held to the halter neck she admired. 'Sure, I've no shoes to go with that shifty yoke.'

'We can easily remedy that.'

'Bronagh, Bobby-Gene's the expert, remember?' Maureen butted in.

'That's right. Trust me.' Bobby-Gene took a step toward Bronagh. 'Give me the dress, Bronagh.' He held his hand out, his tone brooking no argument, but this was Bronagh he was dealing with.

'But Bobby-Gene, would you look at the polka dots? I love the polka dots.' Bronagh hugged the dress to her.

'It's a big, fat no to the polka dots, Bronagh. Would you try the yellow shift dress because you'll look dazzling with your hair and eyes and the pop of turquoise? My God, girl! Leonard won't be able to keep his hands off you.'

He was good, Maureen thought. *Very good*. He knew exactly what buttons to push because Bronagh abandoned the polka dots to sling the yellow shift dress over her arm and patter over to the fitting room to wait her turn.

'And what would you be suggesting for me, Bobby-Gene? I'm partial to the wrap style of dress because it's very flattering where the middle bits are concerned.' Maureen didn't want Bobby-Gene to think she was naïve in the fashion world, even if she had bought a sunflower print dress that made her look like a talking flower.

'Give me a moment, Maureen.'

Maureen watched as he ran his hand over a row of orange dresses. 'In case you didn't know, the BO colour's very last season, so it is.'

'Orange pairs well with hot pink, but,' Bobby-Gene moved on, 'so does lime.' He whisked a green jumpsuit off the rack.

Maureen's mouth worked from side to side, appraising the outfit. 'I was thinking more along the lines of a dress, and don't you think I'd look a little like a Liquorice Allsorts someone's pinched the liquorice from with my scarf wearing that?'

'Maureen, the cut is perfect for your petite frame. See how the waist is elevated?'

She nodded reluctantly.

'That will make your legs look like they go on forever.'

Maureen had always wanted legs that went on forever.

'And the top here is fitted, which will help create a long, lean vertical line. The colour will bring out your tan, and I'm thinking lime heels to create the illusion of height.'

'Alright, so, let me get this straight, Bobby-Gene. What you're saying to me is the lime green jumpsuit will make me look like a taller woman with long, lean legs.'

'I am.' Bobby-Gene confirmed.

'I've always been partial to the Liquorice Allsorts,' Maureen said, holding her hand out for the hanger.

Chapter Twenty-five

A twenty-minute, shoulder-to-shoulder taxi journey brought them to the winery Bobby-Gene had in mind for lunch. It was located above the Port of Athinios, and as they dropped their bags and sat down under the shade of a gnarled, leafy grapevine whose leaves were on the turn, they all agreed it was a good choice. The view of the Caldera was superb. A low wall encompassed the cobbled terrace area where theirs was one of a cluster of tables protecting them from the cliff face, and on the other side of it, rocks jutted out that reminded Maureen of the pumice stone in her shower at home. You had to admire the tenacity of the white and purple flowers sprouting on such unforgiving terrain. She wondered what they were called. Then returning her gaze to the table, she saw Bronagh and Wendy were busy waving out to the cruise ship cutting through the glass waters below while Bobby-Gene was already inspecting the menu.

They didn't have to wait long for their sommelier to introduce herself and discuss the options available. Finally, a four-wine-tasting and luncheon platter was agreed upon after a short round-the-table discussion. Bobby-Gene rubbed his hands together as the wine waiter disappeared inside the taverna part of the winery. 'I'm looking forward to this. We've earned it after what I think was a successful morning.'

'It was,' Maureen agreed, and Wendy and Bronagh nodded along with the sentiment.

'Although, if you'd told me first thing this morning, Bobby-Gene, that I'd be looking forward to a wine-tasting luncheon, I'd have said you were mad.' Bronagh pointed a polished, summery pink fingernail in his direction. 'And I don't mind telling you when you insisted I try on the yellow shift dress, I thought you were mad. It's not the sort of thing I'd gravitate towards.'

'No, I got that. You made it very clear you saw yourself as a polka-dot woman.' Bobby-Gene flashed a grin and, taking his hat off, ran his fingers through mid-brown hair a little longer in the front than at the back. A sheen of sweat made his brow glisten. 'I'm glad we're in the shade.'

Bronagh wasn't finished, however. 'But you were right to say I needed to trust you because you were spot on and once you'd knotted the scarf for me, I could see what you meant. I felt a million dollars in that dress with the silk scarf, so I did, and I love the shoes we found to tie the outfit all together.'

'A satisfied customer, then?' Bobby-Gene plopped his hat back on.

'Very.'

Wendy and Maureen were equally happy with the suggestions Bobby-Gene had made for them, although Maureen was a little perturbed about how she was supposed to go for a wee when wearing the jumpsuit. Did she have to take the whole thing off every time the urge to spend a penny overtook her? It wasn't the sort of thing you could drop in over a slap-up wine-tasting lunch, but if that were the case, then there'd be a lot of leg-crossing going on, which wasn't good at her age. Ah, well, at least she'd look the part. That was the important thing.

'I've spent far too much, but a morning's retail therapy's been good for me,' Wendy joined in. 'I've thoroughly enjoyed myself, so thank you for including me.' She smiled at them all, then added with a shrug, 'I don't know when I'll get the chance to wear my dress, though.'

'Do you need an occasion to feel fabulous?' Bobby-Gene asked.

'I hadn't thought of it like that,' Wendy said.

'Well, while we're on the subject of occasions to wear your dress, Wendy, here's the thing.' Maureen leaned across the table toward her. 'I'll get straight to the point.'

'Please do,' Wendy said, baffled about where this was leading.

'Bronagh and I think you have a soft spot for Georgios.'

'Sorry?' Wendy's face instantly flushed the same hot pink as Maureen's scarf, suggesting she'd heard what Maureen had said loud and clear.

'Myself and Bronagh here; we think you carry a torch for Georgios and he for you, only he's not twigged yet. Men can be a little thick like that.'

'Thanks a lot,' Bobby-Gene said.

Wendy coughed and said, 'I, erm, I—is it that obvious?'

'Not at all.'

'But you two noticed.'

'Ah, but we're perceptive when it comes to matters of the heart, aren't we, Bronagh?'

'We are.' Bronagh's hair swished back and forth like one of those mad pirate ship rides at a fun fair as she nodded enthusiastically. 'I've told you how Leonard and I became a couple. Who knows where the pair of us would be now if Aisling hadn't decided to interfere, but lonely is the word that springs to mind? Sometimes it takes someone on the outside looking in to give two people a nudge in the right direction. Sure, you'd have heard of our Matchmaking Festival in Lisdoonvarna?'

'Erm, no. I can't say that I have.'

'It's a big deal, so it is. People come from all over the world to be matched up by a traditional bona fide matchmaker. My point is though Wendy, Bobby-Gene, Maureen and myself are here to give you and Georgios a nudge in the right direction.'

'I still don't understand.'

'Let me put it this way. Think of us as your fairy godmothers because we're here to help Georgios realise he feels the same way about you as you do about him. Or, to put it figuratively, bang your heads together. We're thinking dinner.'

The plan, which had only been vague, crystalised in Maureen's mind. 'Yes, dinner tomorrow night. My son-in-law, Quinn's a chef, like. He'll cook yourself and Georgios a traditional Irish meal. Bronagh, the girls and I will be on hand as the kitchen staff, so all you have to do is show up looking gorgeous in your dress. That peacock blue was gorgeous on you by the way.'

'It was and that's a grand plan,' Bronagh said, sitting back in her seat, impressed.

'Thank you.'

'I'll do your hair and makeup,' Bobby-Gene said excitedly.

'But why? I mean, why are you doing this?'

'Because I think we have a fair bit in common, you and I.' Maureen confided her story of being widowed and finding love again unexpectedly with Donal, and slowly the stain in the pension owner's cheeks began to fade.

Bobby-Gene listened intently. 'I'd like to know more about this Matchmaker's Festival.'

'We'll sort you in a minute Bobby-Gene.' Maureen flapped her hand at him. 'Right now, we're dealing with Wendy here.'

'That's me told.'

Wendy gave him a wry smile, then looked toward Bronagh, and Maureen said, 'I didn't think I'd ever feel much of anything after Stanley died, but with Georgios, it's crept up on me.'

'A slow burn,' Bronagh said.

'Where'd you get that from, a slow burn?' Maureen asked. 'I like it.'

'The romance novel I brought with me. It's called a slow-burn romance.'

Wendy waited for them to finish. 'The strange thing is it's down to Ana, his late wife. She was lovely and so good to me when I first arrived in Karterados. We became close friends, and it broke my heart when she passed, but before she died, she asked me to watch over Georgios for her. She said she knew he would have Obelia but that it would comfort her to know I'd be there, too.' Then, it was Wendy's turn to explain what had since transpired with Obelia and how father and daughter were estranged.

It explained Georgios's unwillingness to speak of his daughter when she'd chatted to him by the pool the previous afternoon, Maureen thought.

'But enough is enough, and borrowing your turn of phrase, Maureen, I will bang their heads together. They need each other, but Georgios has to accept Obelia is her own person, not an extension of him and Ana, and as such she's a right to lead the life she wants. He's agreed to ring her so long as I help him with what he needs to say to her. He desperately misses her and wants her back in his life, and he won't be happy, properly happy, I mean, until she is.'

'Am I right in thinking that his relationship with Obelia needs to be mended first if he's to let himself see that he doesn't have to be alone?' Maureen probed.

'I think so,' Wendy nodded slowly. 'People need to be happy within themselves before they can be happy with another person.'

'Tis very true,' Bronagh said.

'And how do you think Obelia would feel if her father were to have a new woman in his life? I only ask because my girls were initially odd about Donal and myself, as were his girls, but it all worked out in the end.'

Wendy took a moment to formulate her reply. 'I think Obelia would be relieved, to be honest. It's not been easy for her trying to carve her own path in life when her parents already had things planned out for her. There was a lot of pressure placed on her as their only child. To have someone else in the picture would relieve that pressure.'

The conversation ended as the sommelier reappeared with an eye-popping platter filled with tomatoes, wedges of cheese, salami and prosciutto, toasted bread and deep green olive oil for dipping.

Maureen pretended to listen intently to what she said about the sampling of wine they were each presented with, secretly wishing she'd leave them to dive into the food. A glance at Bronagh all but dribbling as she eyed the cheese suggested she felt the same way. Nevertheless, Bobby-Gene raised his glass and said, '*Yammas*,' which the three women echoed, sipping their wine and making appropriate, fruity yet dry and crisp sort-a comments about the alcoholic beverage that was more golden than white. The minute the woman disappeared to retrieve the next round, which she'd said was a semi-dry rosé, they fell upon the platter. So it was she returned, glasses filled to the appropriate level with a light, pink wine, to a table full of chipmunk-cheeked guests.

Three glasses later and left to their own devices, Bronagh mopped up the dregs of olive oil with the last piece of bread and announced she'd enjoyed the red wine best and might buy a bottle to take back to share with Leonard.

'I liked them all,' Maureen hiccupped.

Bobby-Gene and Wendy agreed with Maureen.

They sat in contented silence for a few minutes soaking in the glorious vista and enjoying having full bellies and enough wine circulating in their systems to loosen tongues but with no danger of the high leg kicking.

It was Bobby-Gene who broke their mediation. 'You know, I have to say, ladies, I've been surprised by your open-mindedness. Maureen, Patrick was uncertain when I came out in full Bobby-Jean style yesterday. Cindy told me quietly he wasn't sure how you'd react.'

'Why did you?' Maureen asked, curious.

'A test. If people can't accept me in all my guises, they're not my kind of folk. You reach a certain age and realise you can't change the world, but you can decide on who you surround yourself with.'

'You'd be right there. And, by the time you've raised four headstrong children, your eyes have been opened wide, so they have, not to mention the lines on your face with the worry and the grey hairs sprouting left, right and centre. As for Pat, he should know myself and Bronagh better than that. Sure, we've seen him heading out the door in all manner of outfits over the years, isn't that right, Bronagh?'

'We have Mo, everything from the Miami Vice shoulder pads to the skin-tight leather trousers. They'd make your eyes water those things, so they would.'

'Jaysus wept. I almost had to snip them off him when he finally agreed to take them off.'

'My sons were the same.' Wendy laughed. 'It's not a person's clothes that matter. It's what's in here.' Wendy laid her hand on her heart.

'Do you steal, Bobby-Gene?' Maureen asked.

Bobby-Gene looked a little affronted by the question. 'Of course not.'

'Well, then, do you go around bopping people for no good reason?'

'No!'

'And, are you the sort-a person who'd give up their seat on a bus for someone who needed it?'

'I don't ride the buses much, but I am.'

'Then you're alright by me, Bobby-Gene.'

'And me,' Bronagh and Wendy were quick to add.

'I think you three are a bit of alright too.' Bobby-Gene gave them a cheeky wink which had them all giggling like teenagers.

'I suppose we should head back to Karterados,' Bronagh said. 'I promised Leonard we'd visit a museum with all ancient artefacts from Santorini in it so long as we've finished in time for a sunset cocktail.'

'Don't tell Donal about that now, will you, or he'll be marching us off there too? We're going to see the Red Beach. What are your plans Bobby-Gene, Wendy?'

'I'm going to thank Leonard, Aisling and Quinn for their help with Stanley's this morning, and then I'm going to convince Georgios to telephone Obelia this evening.'

They all looked to Bobby-Gene. 'This bad boy is going to find a sun lounger and not move from it until it's time to eat again.'

Then, picking up their bags, they said goodbye to their blissful view because they'd things to do and people to see.

Chapter Twenty-six

♥

A small group assembled for dinner in a taverna Georgios had recommended just off the square in Karterados that evening. Maureen, Donal, Noah, Moira, Tom and Kiera, Aisling, Quinn, Aoife and Connor were gathered around a table in a courtyard festooned with tiny, twinkling lights. The potted lemon and mandarin trees gave off a gorgeous aroma, and the night sky was alive with pinprick stars. Roisin and Shay had ventured off for a romantic meal on their own, making the most of having Maureen and Donal available to keep an eye on Noah. So too, had Bronagh and Leonard. A couple was dining in the far corner beside the splash of bougainvillea, and Maureen watched as their meals were carried over by the stout Greek woman who appeared to be multitasking. From what Maureen had seen, she was the hostess and the cook. A whiff of something meaty and hearty made her stomach rumble. It had been quite a strenuous afternoon exploring the Red Beach, and she needed solid sustenance.

'That's very good, Noah,' Maureen said to her grandson, seated to her left. His mother had the foresight to arm him with pen and paper to keep him occupied while he waited for his meal. 'I think you've inherited your Aunty Moira's talent for art there.' She didn't like to say she hadn't a clue what he'd drawn, but it was putting her in mind of a potato with eyes.

'It's a present for Sherry.'

'Lovely.' Maureen smiled. Roisin had mentioned he was pretty taken with Cindy's sister.

'What was the Red Beach like then?' Quinn asked, rocking Connor in his arms. The baby boy was seconds from nodding off by the looks of him, whereas his sister was bright-eyed, gazing up at her mammy.

'It was very good. Well worth a look. I wouldn't recommend taking the twins with you if you decide to visit because the path down to it is rough, but sure, Mo and myself will mind them if you want to go,' Donal said. He took a sip of his beer and, putting it down, drew breath. Maureen swiftly jumped in because she sensed he was gearing up to tell them all about how the red rocks had formed through earthquakes and eruptions and how the colour resulted from iron and sulphuric elements in the ground. She'd heard it all this afternoon as she picked her way down the stony path to the viewing point, not game to carry on down to the beach proper.

'Tis something to see, alright, but if you visit it, you're not to get clever and think the barriers don't apply to you because they're there for a reason, and no child or son-in-law of mine will get hit by falling rocks on this holiday. Understand?'

A general nodding went around the table.

'Kiera's very quiet. She's not sickening for something, I hope?' Maureen pointed to where her granddaughter was perched in a plastic high chair, seemingly mesmerised by the fairy lights strewn about the place. She had her customary spoon in hand but wasn't banging it in her usual frantic 'I'm starving; would you feed me already' manner.

'Maybe we should get fairy lights for her room, Tom?' Moira said.

The woman, whose face was sweaty and red from all the multitasking she was after doing, appeared to take their orders just then, and the menus were hastily flicked open. They didn't faff about ordering because she didn't come across as the sort-a woman who'd smile politely while you debated what to have for dinner.

'How did your morning go, girls?' Maureen asked once the menus had been handed back. She helped herself to a roll from the breadbasket and began to butter it. Her action broke Kiera's trance, and she began banging the spoon until her mammy put a roll on her tray. Noah, too, stopped his potato portrait and asked his Nana if he could have one.

'You'd better eat your dinner, Noah,' she said, passing the basket to him.

'I will, Nana,' he said earnestly. 'Pizza is the best dinner in the whole world.'

Maureen smiled indulgently and waved at Aoife.

'Don't, Mammy. You'll overstimulate her,' Aisling said, covering her daughter's eyes. 'You're to go to sleep now so your Mammy can eat her dinner in her peace.

Maureen remembered her question. 'How did you get on with the dance routine Sherry's after choreographing?'

Aisling and Moira looked at one another. 'We'd rather not talk about it.'

'Oh, dear. You two never were very coordinated, not like Rosi. Baby elephants in tutus the pair of you.'

'I'm coordinated, thanks very much.' Aisling got up and placed Aoife in the pram beside a sleeping Connor. 'Sure, don't you remember me taking the salsa dance lessons? It's how Quinn and I got together.' She exchanged a sappy lovesick look with her husband, then continued. 'Moira couldn't get the hang of the hand movements today.' She proceeded to demonstrate the swirly, weaving movements.

Maureen commented, 'Sure, you look like you're washing the windows.' Then as Aisling got into the swing of it, waving her arms around over her head, she added, 'Put your arms down. We get the idea.'

'It's not my fault I couldn't get into the groove. Madonna's not my era,' Moira muttered.

Aisling wound down the dance moves and apologised to Quinn for thwacking him in the head as she sat back down. 'To be fair, I think we looked more like we were doing the dance of the seven veils than Madonna.'

'Can we not talk about it anymore,' Moira said glumly. 'We'll look like total eejits jigging up the beach like so.'

'I'm looking forward to it. The craic will be mighty,' Tom said, earning a glare that informed him the stables would be shut and there'd be no riding this evening.

Moira eyed her Mammy across the table. 'I like your outfit and the scarf,' Moira said, giving her Mammy a rare compliment as she changed the subject.

'So do I.' Aisling backed her up.

Maureen fluffed her hair. Donal too had been effusive when she'd appeared after going for her final wee before putting the jumpsuit on. 'Wait until you see Bronagh and Wendy dressed up. Bobby-Gene did us all proud.' She'd already explained it had been a very different version of Bobby-Jean or Gene, who'd taken them shopping this morning—different but just as lovely.

'Wendy, as in the woman running the pension where you're staying?' Moira pointed to Aisling, puzzled.

Aisling nodded.

'Have I missed something? Why did she go with you?'

Maureen updated her and the others on the plan where Wendy and Georgios were concerned and, when she'd brought them up to speed, finished by saying, 'So, Quinn, I'm going to need you to cook tomorrow evening.'

'I will, of course, do something traditional to give them a taste of Ireland.'

'And I'll be the waitress,' Aisling got in quick.

'But that means I'll be on washing up.' Moira frowned.

'I got in first.'

'I'll not give you the presents I bought for you if you don't stop your bickering.' Maureen looked from one to the other.

Aisling and Moira's mouths clamped shut, and they looked to their mammy expectantly.

'Do I get a present, Nana?' Noah asked, and Keira shouted, 'Me!'

'Not tonight, I'm afraid, but you can choose any dessert that takes your fancy after your pizza.'

That satisfied the little boy, and tongue poking out the corner of his mouth, he returned to his drawing while Kiera shouted 'Me!' once more.

'And you. You can have dessert, too.' Maureen was rewarded with a baby-toothed grin.

'A-hem,' Aisling cleared her throat to remind her mammy she and Moira were still there.

'Oh yes.' Maureen unhooked her bag off the back of her chair and opened it to retrieve two tissue paper-wrapped packages. 'Now I wrote your initials on them to know whose was whose. Donal, have you seen my glasses?' She put the parcels on the table and patted about for her glasses.

'On your head Mo.'

Maureen gave him a 'What would I do without you' look and slipped them on to peer at the tissue paper. 'Right, this one's yours, Aisling, and this is yours, Moira. I'll give Roisin hers later. I've one for Cindy and Sherry too.'

'Thanks, Mammy,' Aisling said, and Moira repeated the sentiment as they each took their parcels and unwrapped them.

'Oh, it's beautiful,' Aisling held her scarf up. 'I love teal.'

'Is it real silk?' Moira asked, examining her purple scarf.

'It is, Moira.'

'I was born to silk, me.' She draped it around her neck.

Maureen rolled her eyes but was pleased she'd chosen well.

Aisling began giggling.

'What's so funny?' Maureen asked, watching Aisling hold her scarf up so only her eyes were visible, much like Bronagh had in The Silk Shop earlier.

'Moira, do I look mysterious?' She began to flutter her scarf peeking out from behind it, and Moira did the same, laughing, although Aisling sobered quickly and apologised as she flicked the Greek woman carrying a dish of Kleftico with her scarf.

The steaming dish was placed in front of Maureen. It looked delicious, but she would start once the others had theirs. Her mind tracked back to the pension. Georgios was cooking for Wendy that evening, Wendy had told them. And, after they'd eaten, she would see that he sorted the mess he'd made of things with Obelia once and for all. She wondered how they were getting on.

Chapter

Twenty-seven

♥

G eorgios pushed his chair back and patted his stomach. 'I think
I'm getting very good at the grilled chicken if I do say so myself.'

'It was delicious,' Wendy agreed, putting her knife and fork down
on her plate and dabbing her mouth with a paper napkin.

Georgios drained the contents of his glass and, putting it down,
asked, 'Do you remember the first time I prepared this for dinner?'

'How could I forget?' Wendy laughed. 'I had to knock the fork out
of your hand.'

'I didn't know it was still raw in the middle.' He threw his hands up
in the air, grinning.

'Well, it was a good job. I spotted it was still pink and stopped you
when I did, or you'd have been in for a nasty bout of food poisoning.'

'I would,' he agreed.

'Your second attempt wasn't much better from memory.' Wendy's
eyes danced mischievously.

'I was so worried about undercooking the meat, I burnt it.'

'To a crisp.'

They both laughed.

Georgios picked up the bottle of wine, but Wendy gestured for him to put it down. 'What is it?'

'You can have another glass later, but right now, you need your wits about you, Georgios Kyrgios, because you're about to telephone your daughter.'

Georgios paled. 'No, Wendy. I'm not ready.'

'That's not true. You've been ready from the minute Obelia walked out of here shouting she was never coming back.'

Georgios rubbed at his temples, remembering the evening she left.

***

Obelia put her knife and fork down, the sound jarring in the kitchen's quiet and cleared her throat. 'Papa, I've something to tell you.'

Georgios had noticed Obelia pushing the meat and vegetables around on her plate. Ana would have told her to stop playing with it. It wasn't as if it weren't delicious because Obelia was an excellent cook. Ana had made sure of that. His daughter had spent an age labouring over tonight's meal, too, having disappeared early this morning to go to the market to be sure of getting the freshest ingredients. She'd gone to all that trouble, and now she'd barely touched her food. Something was going on. His stomach churned anxiously. The fork with the tender piece of lamb skewered on it was frozen between his mouth and plate because there was something in Obelia's tone warning him he wasn't going to like whatever it was she was about to say. He put the utensil down and waited, tilting his head to one side.

When she saw she had her father's attention, Obelia's words tripped over each other in their haste to get out what had to be said. 'I'm not staying here in Santorini, Papa. I'm returning to Athens tomorrow to start work at the Four Seasons, Hotel.'

Georgios stared blankly across the table at her. She'd only been home a week after finishing her hospitality studies, and now she was talking about leaving. He couldn't make sense of what she'd said.

'Papa, please say something.'

Georgios tried to formulate a coherent sentence, but it came out as jumbled as his thoughts. 'No.' He shook his head. 'I don't understand. You can't go back to Athens.'

'Please try and understand,' Obelia said, but he cut her off.

'No, Obelia. You're staying here. You know this. For you to run Kyrgios's with me is what your *mána* wanted.'

'But you and *mána* never asked me what I wanted.' Obelia's voice cracked.

'This is your home.' Georgios banged his fist on the table, having had enough of this silliness. 'It is where you belong.'

'I want more than this island, Papa. It's a big world.'

Georgios gave a dismissive snort. 'What do you know of the world? You're only nineteen, a child still. Enough of this, Obelia, you are making my head hurt.' He rubbed a hand over his forehead to prove his point. He didn't see his adult daughter sitting across from him for a moment, but the determined little girl with her hair in bunches and two missing front teeth.

'I'm going tomorrow, Papa.' There was a set to her jaw that signalled her resolve.

'You will break your *mána's* heart if you leave Obelia.'

'Papa, *mána* isn't here anymore. I don't want to live here with her ghost. I loved her as much as I love you, but she's gone, and I must live my life. It's not my fault if you won't move on and live yours.'

Georgios head snapped back then as though he'd been slapped. 'How dare you speak to me this way! And if you leave, then you don't come back.'

'Papa, please, I'm sorry. Try to understand!' Obelia's dark eyes, so like her late mother's, flashed with frustration and fear. Her father meant what he said as she scraped her chair back from the table and stood up. 'Don't make me choose.'

***

'Georgios?'

Wendy was speaking to him, Georgios realised, blinking the past away.

'What will I say, Wendy?'

'You'll say you're sorry. You understand and that you love and miss her.' She smiled her encouragement.

'You will stay while I make this call?' There was a pleading light in Georgios's eyes.

'I'll be right by your side. I promise.'

Georgios got up from the table then and took a slow, steadying breath before moving to the front of the pension. He was too antsy to sit at the reception desk, and picking up the phone, he tapped out the number he'd committed to memory after his last failed attempt to speak to his daughter.

His stomach flipped over, waiting for Obelia to answer, and Wendy took hold of his free hand, he grasped it tightly as if it were a lifeline.

'*Yassou?*'

Georgios looked at Wendy, his eyes wide.

She mouthed. 'I'm sorry. I understand. I love and miss you.'

'Obelia, it is your papa.'

'Papa?'

He heard the sob catch in his daughter's throat, and his eyes burned but blinking the threatened tears away, he said, 'I'm sorry. I understand. I love and miss you very much.'

Chapter Twenty-eight

♥

'Maureen, you and Donal are to stand on the bride and groom's right with Tom, Quinn and the babies,' a tanned, bikini-clad Sherry bossed with a flick of her tousled locks. They were gathered under a cloudless sky on Kamari Beach for the wedding rehearsal, which Sherry, in her head bridesmaid capacity, had informed them was so that everyone was clear about where they were to position themselves for the service, proper tomorrow.

'You can just imagine her bossing all those poor wee children at her dance class,' Maureen said out the corner of her mouth as she and Donal did as they were told, their feet sinking into the hot, black mix of sandy shingle. *It was picturesque*, she thought, scanning the beach. The rock rearing out of the water over there like so would make a grand backdrop for the wedding photographs. Those jet skiers parading back and forth on their water mobiles had better think twice about revving their engines tomorrow. It was a shame they were too far away for her to use the 'look'.

Sherry moved on, shuffling Shay along, and Maureen marvelled over how her breasts stayed contained within the tiny pieces of fabric doing such a poor job of covering them. Then, seeing Tom and Quinn were also marvelling, she fixed them with the 'look'. The two men busied themselves, arranging their offspring's sun hats. But, bless him, Donal was inspecting the shale granules he'd picked up. She mused that he could have been a geologist in another life, staring past him to see they were drawing curious stares from those strolling along the water's edge. A bronzed, oil-slick couple who, for some reason, made her think of Tarzan and Jane were presently gawping over at them.

'Okay, y'all looking good,' Sherry said with satisfaction as her blue eyes flicked over everybody to ensure she'd positioned them where she wanted them for the wedding.

That was subject to opinion, Maureen thought, glad of her floaty beach cover-up. Ciara had done her proud with that, at least. There was nothing wrong with leaving a little to the imagination, she always thought and hoped Bea wasn't planning on wearing her plunging one-piece tomorrow. It was now apparent where Cindy and Sherry got their love of all things barely-there from. Later, she'd be sending up a prayer for Big Jim to have the sense to put a shirt and shorts on tomorrow for the sake of the photos. For goodness sake, he wasn't German or about to compete in the Olympics. Why could he not have worn the board shorts? Tom and Quinn weren't the only ones on the receiving end of the 'look'. She'd had to fix the girls with a glare earlier to nip any potential smart-arse remarks or inappropriate giggling at Patrick's soon-to-be father-in-law's poor underpants masquerading as swimwear choice in the bud. As for Bronagh, also a lover of the floaty coverall, her eyes had nearly popped out of her head catching sight of Big Jim, and looking at her and Leonard now, she wasn't surprised to see he'd opted to wear his socks and sandals to the beach.

Maureen turned her attention to the happy couple. They were standing in matching shorty, white beach robes with an embroidered 'A W', presumably for Azure Waters on their backs, compliments of the resort, with Bobby-Gene wisely clad in board shorts in front of them. On their left were Shay, Bronagh and Leonard, having been told to stand on the bride's family side to even up the numbers. Shay, thinking no one was looking, was edging away from Bea. Maureen thought he was a sensible lad, her gaze not lingering for long on Bea and Big Jim as it skipped to Sherry. She was bending down to speak to Noah, and there was a strong possibility of fall-out. Maureen only began breathing again once she saw things had stayed where they should. If Noah paid as much attention to his teachers in years to come as he was to Sherry's chest, he'd be top of the class!

Roisin, Aisling and Moira were the last to be hustled into line. They were put in age formation and looked prudish in their swimsuits for a change compared to Sherry. As the buxom blonde told them they'd not be doing the dancing because it was to be a surprise for the groom, all three girls' shoulders sagged with relief at the reprieve.

'If you need to run through it a couple more times, I'm available this afternoon,' Sherry added.

'No, not at all. I've got the moves down pat,' Moira said, pulling her bathers out of her bottom.

'Me, too,' Aisling assured her.

'It's all up here.' Roisin tapped the side of her head.

Satisfied, Sherry told them they were dismissed, and the wedding party made their way over to the rows of palm leaf-shaded sun loungers. Upon hearing the charge for the privilege of lounging, Donal consulted his guidebook and herded them down to an empty cluster of recliners in front of a restaurant straddling the beach. 'These are free so long as we use the restaurant.'

'No problem there, Doe-nell. I'm starving.' Big Jim waddled toward the restaurant while the others settled themselves in for the next few hours at least.

***

Maureen had lost track of time as she stretched out on the plastic lounger feeling the towel bunching under her. The book she'd brought rested across her chest, and the breeze blowing down the beach ensured she was at the perfect temperature. A sense of sleepy contentment stole over her as it had Donal, who was giving off rumbling snores from the lounger next to hers. Through heavy-lidded eyes, she glanced around, seeing Bronagh sipping a multi-coloured concoction through a straw nearby. She recalled their earlier conversation about Georgios. He'd been whistling as he refilled the coffee over breakfast, and Wendy confided to Bronagh that he'd telephoned his daughter the night before, and things had gone well. Maureen felt an anticipatory twinge that this evening's meal should go just as well.

'Nana!' Noah called out to her.

He was sitting on a towel, with Kiera digging for Africa.

'Where did you get the spade, Noah?' Maureen asked. 'Kiera, don't be putting the sand in your mouth.'

'I found it.'

'Are you looking for treasure?'

'Pirates' gold, and I won't be sharing it with Kiera because all she's doing is eating sand. She's not helping at all,' the little boy huffed and puffed.

'Well, good luck to you. Moira, would you stop your child from eating the sand and feed her something.'

'Tom! Kiera's eating sand again.' Moira nudged him.

Lazy mare, Maureen thought, nudging Donal. He gave a particularly virulent snort and jolted awake. 'Good, you're awake.'

'I was only resting my eyes.'

'Noah's after digging for pirates' gold. Why don't you take him down for a splash about in the sea, and I'll bury a couple of coins there for him to find?'

Donal chuckled. 'I like the way you think, Mo.' He eased himself off the lounger. 'Noah, you've been working hard there, I see.'

'I have Poppa D.'

'How about taking a break and keeping an eye on me while I take a dip in the water there.'

Noah abandoned his spade. 'Hold my hand Poppa D. I'm a good swimmer, aren't I, Mummy?'

'Yes, you are, although it doesn't pay to get cocky, Noah. You've to respect the water.'

Noah placed Poppa D's meaty paw in his hand and trotted off down to the water. Maureen didn't waste any time retrieving a few shiny coins from her purse, and when the little boy was engrossed in splashing about, she snuck over to his dig site and buried them. Kiera she saw was sitting on her daddy's tummy, eating a banana pilfered from the fruit bowl at breakfast, so there was no chance of her trying to scoff them.

Roisin watched her with amusement. 'He'll be beside himself when he finds that, Mammy.'

'Be sure to have your camera ready,' Maureen said, sitting back down.

'I will.'

They had to wait a good twenty minutes for the duo to venture back up the beach, and Roisin, towel at the ready, wrapped Noah in it, who declared himself 'starving'.

'I tell you what, why don't you go back to your digging there for five more minutes and then we'll go and see about lunch. Does that sound like a good plan?'

Noah nodded, and Roisin grinned at Shay and then winked at her mammy as he picked the spade up once more and returned to it. She slipped her camera out of her bag and got ready.

'Gold! I've found gold!' Noah shouted a second later, clambering to his feet and holding two coins aloft. He ran over to his mum, who was clicking away to show her and Shay, then to his Nana and Poppa D, who were beaming from ear to ear.

'Isn't that grand, Noah.' Maureen said.

'Me!' Kiera shouted, and Noah pursed his lips, looking wise beyond his years as he marched over to his cousin.

'Bless. Noah's going to give Kiera one of the coins. Ah, seeing the bond those two have melts my heart,' Maureen said. 'Although, she'll not be happy when her mammy takes the coin off her. You know what Kiera's like. She'll try and eat it. She's her mammy's attitude and Aunty Aisling's appetite that one.'

Noah's voice travelled on the breeze toward Maureen and Donal, ringing out clear as a bell. 'I'm sorry, Kiera, but if you don't work hard, you can't expect to get paid.' He pocketed both coins.

'He'll make a shrewd boss one day, so he will, Mo,' Donal said, laughing.

Chapter Twenty-nine

♥

Q uinn set the shopping bag full of ingredients he'd need for the Irish stew, mashed potato and the soda bread he'd put his mind to making down on Georgios's kitchen worktop and flexed his hand. It had cramped from lugging the bag back from the small family-run supermarket Georgios had pointed him in the direction of.

Maureen hadn't messed about, taking charge on their return to the pension after hours whiled away at the beach to inform their unsuspecting host that her son-in-law, a chef, no less, would be preparing himself and Wendy's dinner that evening. They were in for a treat, she'd informed him, and a taste of Ireland. When Georgios had protested that it was a kind and generous thought, but it wouldn't be right given they were his and Wendy's paying guests, Maureen had held her hand up and informed him it would be Quinn's pleasure to do so. 'Won't it, Quinn?' She turned to her son-in-law, who backed her up.

'Think of me as a culinary ambassador for my country,' Quinn said before asking where he'd find a supermarket.

Georgios, who knew a determined woman when he saw one and a son-in-law who was under her thumb, decided he would be wasting his breath if he bothered to protest further. He'd pointed Quinn toward Thira Foods, his local.

Now, here Quinn was, unpacking the groceries feeling pleased to have found everything necessary for the dish. It shouldn't be surprising, given he'd chosen it for its lack of complicated ingredients. Once everything was set out, he'd familiarise himself with the kitchen before getting down to the nitty-gritty of preparing the meal, and a glance at the clock told him he had just over an hour and a half to get it ready.

He was nothing if not a professional, and forty minutes later, the meat was simmering in its broth, and the potatoes were waiting to be brought to the boil in the pan. His floured hands were plunged into a bowl of sticky dough, ready to give it a rough knead, when Maureen ducked her head in the kitchen to see how he was getting on.

'The stew smells wonderful, Quinn. Sure, Aisling hit the jackpot by marrying a man who can cook. Do you need a hand?' She wondered over the orderliness of the worktop. Her son-in-law had cleaned up as he went along and seemed to have everything in hand. The table was set, and he'd even opened a bottle of wine to let it breathe. *The only thing missing was flowers*, she thought, deciding to go and snip a few from the pot she'd seen out the front of the pension. A splash of colour would be the finishing touch on the table.

'No. You're grand, Maureen. There's only the bread to be seen too. I'll be dishing up on the dot of seven as we planned.'

'Well done, Quinn. Oh, and by the way, we won't starve either. Shay and Tom are going into the square to pick up some pizzas for our dinner once everything's underway. After that, we'll all congregate around the pool to eat. Now you haven't come across a pair of scissors, have you?'

'There's some in that top drawer there.' Quinn inclined his head toward it, not asking what she needed them for.

Maureen crossed the room and opened the drawer, rifling through the jumble of utensils until she found what she was looking for. 'Back in a tick.' She headed off. She thought it was another beautiful evening, stepping outside to be greeted by the ginger, white cat who began meowing frantically. 'Have you not been fed then?' Maureen asked, spying the empty bowl. There was more mewling. 'Well, that's not good enough, is it now? I'll be having a word with Georgios on your behalf, so I will.' A phone began ringing from inside the pension as the cat brushed about her legs, and for a moment, she felt a pang for Pooh. How was he getting on without her and Donal? At least Rosemary had the best of Kenny Roger's CD if he was unsettled, she mused, before inspecting the colourful pot. She snipped a stem filled with plump, red blooms, which she automatically held to her nose. It was a scent that reminded her of roses and lemons, making her smile.

Georgios was at his desk scribbling in his fat reservation book on her return. He had a computer which he'd already informed her he didn't trust, using the old-fashioned handwritten method for backup. Bronagh was the same. He glanced up, registering the flowers Maureen was holding and looked at her quizzically.

'They're for the table,' she explained as Georgios shook his head, giving her the impression he was baffled as to what all the fuss over this dinner was about. 'Oh, and you've got a starving cat out there.'

'He's not my cat,' Georgios said, retrieving the box of cat biscuits, he kept under the desk.

'If you're feeding him, he's yours,' Maureen said, leaving him to it.

The tall glass tumbler did the job, and she set her improvised vase down on the table, surveying it with satisfaction. Her eyes flitted over to the wall clock. It was six-forty. 'Seeing as you've everything under control here, Quinn, I'm going to duck next door to see how Bob-by-Gene's getting on with Wendy. He's on hair and makeup.' She was itching to see Wendy's transformation and wanted to pin Bobby-Gene down regarding her eyebrows. Quinn didn't look up from where he was shaping his mound of dough on a floured tray as he said, 'Cheerio'.

***

'Hello there,' Maureen called out, closing the door behind her as she stepped inside Stanley's. 'In here, Maureen.' Bronagh's voice drifted out from the depths of the pension, and Maureen navigated her way towards her friend's voice, suspecting, Bronagh, Bobby-Gene, and Wendy were in the kitchen. She was right, and it was easy to find, given the pension was a similar layout to Georgios's. Unlike Georgios's, though, there were no enticing aromas that promised a delicious meal but rather the chemically sweet scent of hairspray mingling with perfume. She appraised the scene. Wendy was positioned on a chair under the light. Her eyes were closed while Bobby-Gene, eyeshadow kit in hand, flicked a brush about with a look of concentration on his face. Bronagh was watching his handiwork intently from where she was standing with her head tilted, hand resting on her chin, off to one side.

'You're just in time, Mo.' Bronagh beckoned her over. 'Bob-by-Gene's nearly finished.'

'Hi Maureen,' Wendy said, her eyes still shut.

Intent on his shading, Bobby-Gene made a noise that Maureen interpreted as a greeting.

'How are things going next door?' Bronagh asked in a hushed voice that suggested a maestro was at work.

Taking Bronagh's cue, Maureen lowered her voice, 'Quinn's got it all coming together nicely. You'll be eating for seven, Wendy. He's after making Irish stew and soda bread, and it smells wonderful.'

'It sounds delicious, Maureen,' Wendy replied. 'But I hope he hasn't gone to all that trouble for nothing because I'm feeling as though I won't be able to eat a bite right now. I'm far too nervous.'

'Ah, no. Shall I fetch Roisin to do a few rounds of the yoga breathing with you?'

'I don't think that will help. It's so silly, given I've been sharing my evening meal with Georgios all this time. Tonight feels different, though.'

'Because it is different.' Bronagh pointed out the obvious. Wendy having her hair and makeup tended to by a professional stylist was not part of her usual evening ritual.

'Alright, a sweep of mascara, and you'll be good to go.' Bobby-Gene was only half listening to their conversation. 'You can open your eyes now.' He wiped away the tiny flecks of bronze eyeshadow underneath Wendy's eyes with a cotton bud. Then, fossicking about in the battered cosmetic bag presumably belonging to Wendy, he produced a mascara staring at the tube, aghast. 'Good God, girl, how old is this?'

Wendy pinkened and then shrugged. 'A few years. Most days, I barely remember a swipe of lipstick.'

Bobby-Gene tutted, 'It will have to do.' Then pumping the wand a few times held it just beneath her lash line and told her to look up and down. 'All that's left to do now,' Bobby-Gene said, returning the wand to the tube, is to take this off. He dropped the mascara back in the makeup bag, removed the black headband holding Wendy's hair back from her face, then fluffed about with the waves he'd teased into shape with a curling wand before taking a step back.

'Beautiful,' he declared.

Bronagh and Maureen eyed his artistry. Wendy still looked like Wendy, only a fresher, more vibrant version with fabulous hair.

'You look gorgeous, and you'd hardly know you'd any makeup on,' Bronagh said.

Maureen agreed with the sentiment.

'Well, I definitely do have makeup on.' Wendy laughed. 'It feels strange.'

'Here, see for yourself.' Bobby-Gene passed her a powder compact, and Wendy flicked it open, examining her face from different angles under the glare of light. 'I was worried I wouldn't look like myself and Georgios would take fright, but you're a marvel Bobby-Gene. Thank you.'

'I'm happy to assist in playing cupid.' He grinned and then, glancing at his wristwatch, said, 'You had better go and get dressed.'

'Where's Aisling?' Maureen asked, looking about as though she might be hiding.

'In their room, seeing to the twins,' Bronagh supplied.

Maureen remembered her eyebrows. 'Bobby-Gene, would you take a look at these for me.' She wiggled her barely-there brows before passing the eyebrow pencil she'd pocketed earlier over.

***

'Will I do?' Wendy asked, standing shyly in the doorway dressed in her peacock blue dress with the emerald green pashmina wrapped elegantly around her shoulders. On her feet were strappy, flat gold sandals.

Maureen, admiring her new-look brows, put the compact down and clapped her hands in delight. Bronagh beamed, and Bobby-Gene had the self-satisfied smile of a man whose work was done.

'It's not too much?'

'Not at all,' Maureen said.

'It's exactly right,' Bronagh agreed.

Bobby-Gene looked affronted at her doubting his efforts.

'Sorry, I'm just not used to wearing makeup.' Wendy pulled an apologetic face for his benefit, then clasping her hands so tightly they could see the whites of her knuckles said, 'I am doing the right thing, aren't I? What if he doesn't feel the same about me as I do him, and I ruin our friendship?'

'Trust us. He does,' Maureen said confidently.

'Nothing ventured, nothing gained,' Bronagh added.

'Life's too short to look back with what ifs, Wendy,' Bobby-Gene finished.

'You're right.' Wendy gave them a brave smile.

'You'll be grand,' Maureen said.

'This time tomorrow, you'll thank us for guiding you in the right direction,' Bronagh said.

'Enough with the chit-chat. Off you go.' Bobby-Gene pushed Wendy gently out the door, not giving her a chance to change her mind and back out.

Chapter Thirty

♥

Georgios sat at the table, sipping the glass of wine Quinn had placed in front of him pensively. It was a peculiar feeling to be sitting here watching the young Irishman putting the finishing touches to the meal he'd prepared. It was almost as if he were sitting in a taverna instead of his kitchen. Peculiar but not in an unpleasant way, he decided, sniffing the air. The fresh soda bread from the oven gave off that tantalising aroma unique to home baking as it cooled on the worktop. He had another swig of his drink, and his eyes grazed over the flowers on the table. A nice touch on Maureen's part, and then with an anxious glance at the clock saw Wendy would be here any minute. So why was he on edge?

On cue, there was a tap at the door. It creaked open, and he put his wine glass down, feeling like the leading man in a film as he gazed at the woman who'd materialised before him. She was familiar and yet an elegant stranger who looked out of place in his humble kitchen.

'Wendy?'

'Of course, it's me,' Wendy said, but even her tinkling laugh sounded different tonight.

Was she nervous? he wondered, his stomach flip-flopping for reasons he couldn't fathom. Something was different. Something was going to change.

Quinn's clearing of his throat reminded him he was a gentleman first and foremost and, as such, should greet his guest accordingly. He got up from the table, feeling a sharp twist in his gut as it dawned on him why she'd gone to so much trouble with her appearance. She must have arranged to meet someone later this evening. He was a fool to have thought for those few glorious seconds that the effort Wendy had gone to this evening was for his benefit.

'You look beautiful,' he managed to say as he touched her bare upper arms and leaned down to kiss her cheek. Her perfume was intoxicating. It was as if his senses, having been dulled through the pain of loss, were slowly switching back on, and he was acutely aware of the heat emanating from her body and its proximity to his. Nor did he want to release her as he thought of how he'd come to rely on Wendy's company. He was comfortable in her presence, and since Ana's death, they'd settled into easy routines he'd thought suited them both, but he was anything but comfortable now. The fog had lifted, and he realised Wendy had always looked beautiful to him. What a fool he'd been for not acknowledging how he felt about her sooner.

'Thank you.' Wendy's voice was soft.

He released her then, and his arms fell loosely to his sides. An awkwardness stretched between them as they stood there, unsure of what to do or say. Georgios couldn't stop himself from blurting what was on his mind, 'Are you going out after dinner?'

'No.' Wendy frowned. 'Why would I be? I am out.'

Quinn announced he was plating up then, and Georgios might like to seat Wendy and see to her wine.

'Yes, of course.' Georgios went through the motions like a teenager on his first date, and Wendy had only just sat down when there was another knock on the door. This time Shay slunk in.

'Don't mind me. I'm under orders from Maureen and Bronagh.'

He was carrying a portable sound system. 'I brought this over to use at Patrick and Cindy's wedding,' Shay explained in the second before Schuman filled the room.

As quickly as he'd arrived, Shay was gone, and Wendy picked up her wine glass. '*Yammas.*'

'*Yammas.*' The ordinariness of the simple toast they said most nights eased Georgios's jitteriness.

Quinn put their meals down in front of them, and they thanked him, gushing over how delicious it looked and smelt. Georgios's fixated on the yellow orbs of butter sinking into the slices of soda bread on the last plate Quinn set down on the table before telling them to enjoy. And then they were alone.

The sounds of their cutlery as they pushed their food about the plate seemed exaggerated, and Georgios surreptitiously watching Wendy knew neither of them was doing the meal the justice it deserved. The time for procrastination had to end, he decided, putting his knife and fork down before pushing his chair back and getting to his feet. 'Would you care to dance?' He held his hand toward Wendy, trying to steady it, and was relieved when she placed hers in his and stood up to join him. They moved together as one, and he positioned one hand on the small of the back, gently guiding her about the kitchen.

'We fit, Georgios.' Wendy's voice was muffled against his chest.

'We do.' His voice was filled with wonder as any last vestiges of awkwardness at the sudden shifting in their relationship vanished.

Georgios stopped moving then, and Wendy tilted her head up so they were looking at one another. Their eyes softened, melting into one another, and when their lips met, they both knew they were where they belonged—with each other.

**

Maureen was sitting in bed rubbing lavender-scented lotion in her hands while Donal ran through his nightly motions in the bathroom. Her novel was on the bedside table, waiting for her to snuggle down and read it, but she knew it was pointless. Her mind was too full of wondering how Georgios and Wendy's evening had gone. And, of course, she was fizzing with excitement over the wedding. Her son would be a married man this time tomorrow evening, and her sigh was both nostalgic and a little sad at the thought of this because it was true what people said about time going by too fast.

She examined her nails, having painted them rosy pink to match the V-necked, cap-sleeved, just-below-the-knees satin dress with lace over-lay she'd finally decided on. She'd sparkly sandals and a fascinator for her hair which mercifully hadn't been flattened in her suitcase. She'd have liked to have worn a hat. Maureen loved a hat, but Moira had convinced her it would be overkill unless it were of the sunhat variety. Bobby-Gene had assured her earlier after they'd stuffed themselves on pizza, and she dragged him upstairs to see her outfit that Ciara had got it right this time. *It was just as well the dress wasn't clingy*, she thought with a guilty twinge at the memory of all that cheese.

An urgent tapping saw her forget about the pizza overindulgence as she tossed the sheet aside and padded over to the door expecting it to be one of the girls. She hoped nothing was wrong with any of her girls or their offspring.

However, it wasn't Moira, Aisling or Roisin standing in the hall. It was Patrick.

Maureen's eyes, smudged with the remains of the mascara she'd done a slapdash job removing, widened with alarm. 'I thought you were laying low tonight at your hotel? Is Cindy alright? The baby?' The blood began rushing in her ears as she looked past her son to see if Cindy was with him.

'Cindy and the baby are fine, Mammy. She's back at our hotel. I told her I was going for a walk.'

Maureen's shoulders sagged as she sent up a silent thank you before studying her son and noting he had the same antsy demeanour she recognised from his youth. Something was up. 'You'd better come in.' She opened the door wider and ushered Patrick in.

The sound of water running followed by gargling signalled Donal was still otherwise occupied as mother and son stood opposite one another.

'What's going on, Pat?' Maureen crossed her arms over her chest in readiness for whatever he was about to say because her mother's intuition which never let her down, told her she wouldn't like it.

'I don't think I can go through with the wedding, Mammy.' He ran his hand through his hair, and Maureen suspected he'd had it highlighted, seeing blonde streaks she'd not noticed before. He was pale beneath his tan, too. 'I'm not ready to get married.'

Maureen snorted, and Patrick took a wary backwards step. *Holy God Above Tonight*, she thought as the rose-tinted glasses she'd always worn when it came to her son slid off. He'd always been fickle, flitting from one thing to the next, but there was no flitting when a baby was involved. Her grandchild. It hurt her to admit it, but her son was selfish, a trait he'd not inherited from either of his parents. 'Now you listen to me, Patrick O'Mara. You're to be a father, and that's the biggest commitment of them all. Are you going to tell me you're not ready for that either?'

'Mammy, don't shout at me,' Patrick pleaded. 'I didn't come here for that.'

'What did you expect? Me to rub your back and say, there, there, sure it's not a bother, son? Well, let me tell you, it is a great big fecking bother!'

Patrick's head whipped back as though she'd slapped him at her swearing, but she wasn't done yet.

'You're a grown man, so you need to face up to your responsibilities.'

The bathroom door opened then, and Donal taking in Maureen's irate features and the shocked face on Patrick, merely smiled and greeted him. 'Hello there, Patrick.'

'Donal,' Patrick mumbled.

Maureen was relieved Donal had put his pyjamas on, deciding against going alfresco this evening. 'Donal, Pat's after telling me he doesn't think he can go through with the wedding, and I'm after telling him it's a bit bloody late to be calling it off and that he should have thought about whether he was ready to commit to Cindy before he tossed the rubber johnnies in the rubbish bin.'

'You didn't actually say that Mammy,' Patrick corrected, turning to Donal. 'She never mentioned the rubber johnny thing.' He shut his mouth as his mammy glared at him.

'Ah, now Patrick, sure, you'd not be the first man to get cold feet the night before his wedding,' Donal said lightly.

'Would he not?' Maureen asked, swallowing down the rant on the tip of her tongue and grasping the glimmer of hope that this was an easily remedied situation, as Donal's easy-breezy tone would suggest.

'Not at all.'

Patrick looked to Donal as though he'd thrown him a lifesaver. 'I'm not?'

'Of course not. There are plenty of good men who've gone before you who got the wobbles about committing themselves for life to another person. Myself included.' Donal gestured to the chair by the window. 'Why don't you take a load off.'

Patrick did so, flopping down in it while Donal sank next to Maureen on the end of the bed.

'I remember feeling like you are now the night before my late wife, Ida, and I said our vows.'

Maureen thought Donal's situation had been different to Pat's, given he was a man of twenty when he got married, not a middle-aged playboy like her son. But then, her mind switched to Brian. Did he have doubts before their wedding? There'd been none on her part. She'd never know if Brian had questioned marrying her, not now, and what did it matter if he had? What mattered was they'd had a happy life together. Patrick and Cindy would, too, if her eejit firstborn could get over himself and grow up.

'You did?' Patrick was asking now.

Donal nodded. 'I'd all but convinced myself I was about to make a terrible mistake and call the whole thing off, but then I tried to imagine my life without Ida in it. And, the thing was, Patrick, I couldn't, and I didn't want to either. It dawned on me in the wee hours when I was tossing and turning that I wasn't having second thoughts because I didn't want to marry her, it was because I was frightened of not measuring up as a husband.'

Patrick was nodding slowly.

'How do you feel when you are with Cindy?'

'Happy apart from when she has me on a diet, but now she's eating for two, life's good.'

'And how would you feel if you were to get back to that hotel of yours and she was to tell you she was calling the wedding off and that you'd be doing your fathering part-time?'

Patrick looked stricken.

'So there you go, son, the look on your face says it all. It's a commitment you'll be making tomorrow, but sure, you've already made it in your heart and head. You're just voicing that to Cindy and your family tomorrow is all.'

'And God,' Maureen added. 'Don't forget he'll be listening in.'

All the tension had seeped from Patrick's shoulders, and he stopped clasping and unclasping his hands as he stared at Donal as though he were the Messiah.

Donal rubbed his hands together in a 'Well now that's sorted' manner, and the bed creaked as he stood up. 'Right then, how about I sort a taxi to get you back to your hotel before Cindy starts worrying about where you've got to?'

Patrick nodded and got to his feet, shoving his hands in his trouser pockets. 'Thanks, Donal.' His tone was genuine.

Maureen, knowing her son had frowned upon another man entering his mammy's life, also relaxed. The wedding would go ahead, and Patrick and Cindy would be fine. A warm glow suffused her because just as she'd accepted Cindy was to be part of her son's life and her family, Patrick had finally done the same where Donal was concerned.

He was a good man, was her Donal.

Chapter Thirty-one

The colourful group converged under a cloudless, blue canopy on the same beach patch where Sherry had whipped them all into line the day before. They'd taken their allocated places with Bobby-Gene at the helm, who had a tight hold of the notes for the service as they fluttered in the breeze. The sea provided a gently lapping backdrop as he winked at Maureen reassuringly. She attempted a smile back, thinking how strange it was to have a man dressed in a baggy white shirt and casual beige pants with matching slip-on shoes in charge of marrying a couple.

She'd had a quiet word in his ear a few minutes earlier, needing to be reassured that despite the lack of holy vestments, papal slippers included, Patrick and Cindy, would still be legally married at the end of the service. Bobby-Gene eased her concerns just as he had with her mother-of-the-groom outfit.

Maureen mused that you'd never know the Patrick standing in front of Bobby-Gene wearing a billowing shirt the same blinding white as his teeth was the same man who'd fronted up at his mammy's hotel last night. Today he looked relaxed with one hand thrust in his trousers pocket in a casual stance. The trousers were also white and baggy, rolled up at the bottoms. She mentally tutted over how he'd gone from one extreme to the other; one minute, it had been sprayed-on leather trousers, the next, a pair that would keep you airborne if you decided to throw yourself from a plane. Ah, well, life was one big series of stages and phases. A lock of hair fell across his forehead, and Maureen itched to wet it and smooth it away as she'd done when he was a child but kept her hands to herself. Instead, she glanced down at her dress, enjoying how the satin shimmered beneath the delicate lace in the sunlight. She touched her fascinator, reassuring herself it was still sitting where it should be.

Maureen wasn't sure whether she was nervous, anxious or excited, suspecting she was a mix of all the three, and she turned toward Donal, who'd trimmed his beard this morning. He looked very handsome, and appraising his shirt, she fiddled with his collar, which needed no fiddling with. He'd gone with the pale blue shirt and chino pants because the Hawaiian-style shirt he'd initially laid out had been too busy, in Maureen's opinion. The red hibiscus flowers on a yellow background would be all you'd see looking at the wedding photos, she'd told him earlier as they got ready. The bride was supposed to be the star of the show, not Donal in his Hawaiian shirt. He'd taken her comments with his usual good cheer, and now he took hold of her hand. She was lucky to have a man in tune with her feelings and squeezed his hand back. What was the time? Should the bridal party be here by now? She hoped the limousine driving them here hadn't got a flat tyre.

Twenty minutes earlier, Georgios had deposited herself, Donal, Tom, Quinn, Shay, Bronagh, Leonard and the babbies here at the beach. He and Wendy, whom she'd noted gleefully, were holding hands as they hung back with the ever-growing crowd of spectators eager for the bride's appearance. As for Bea, Big Jim and Bobby-Gene, well, she had no idea how they'd got here.

Bobby-Gene gave Maureen a wink, and she smiled back and then looked to where Bronagh was holding hands with Leonard. Love was in the air, alright. She looked very well in her shift dress and silk scarf, having opted to wear her new purchases saying the dress she'd brought over with her to wear today was a little snug around the middle. 'It's the menopause. It gives me terrible bloating,' she'd told Wendy as she exited the pension that morning. *Never mind her appetite for cocktails and deep-fried calamari*, Maureen had thought fondly. Leonard was wearing a loose linen shirt and trousers. Maureen suspected Bronagh had revisited the boutique they'd found their dresses in with Bobby-Gene the other day and kitted him out. She'd been unable to get him out of his socks and sandals, though, she saw.

Quinn had Aoife and Connor in a twin baby carrier which had involved a lot of faff to get them into, but they were content snuggled in against their daddy. Kiera was happily slapping her daddy's cheek. All three men, Shay, Tom and Quinn, had done the O'Mara side proud. As for Bea and Big Jim, they were clothed, for which she was grateful, and to be fair, they'd scrubbed up respectably, although Bea did have a look of your Carmen Miranda wan. All that was missing was the fruit bowl on her head and she hoped Big Jim's shirt would hold firm for the duration of the service. The buttons were straining, and it looked to be touch and go.

An excited murmur swept through the gathered beachgoers.

'They're here.' Donal nudged Maureen, who retrieved her camera from her shoulder bag even though Shay had officially been given the task of photographer. She shaded her eyes and watched as the suit-clad, cap-wearing driver helped Cindy out of the stretched car. Sherry, Roisin, Aisling and Moira emerged next, while Noah, a mini version of Patrick all in white, was the last to appear. He was under strict instructions from his mammy that he wasn't to eat or drink until after the service.

'Don't they look a picture,' Maureen said, blinking rapidly. Bronagh, she saw, was doing the same, and the two women exchanged a complicit tearful smile. A glance at her son revealed he'd puffed up with pride at the sight of his blooming yet strangely virginal-looking, pregnant bride.

Sherry soon had the bridal party in order, and then as they stepped onto the beach with Cindy leading the way, no bouquet in hand, she popped her head around the bride's generous girth and flapped her hand at Shay. Maureen thought that if she were holding a flag, she'd have looked like she was waving off the Formula One racers. Shay took his cue and pressed play on the sound system he'd also been charged with. *He was a very good multitasker, was Shay*, Maureen thought.

Madonna's 'Into the Groove' began to belt out, and the crowd cheered as Cindy struck a pose before raising her arms over her head and twirling her way across the shaley foreshore to the claps of the sun-worshipping onlookers. Roisin, Aisling and Moira followed suit, and nobody minded that Moira kept twirling the wrong way. Noah, with intense concentration on his face, walked behind his Aunties with the rings on a white velvet cushion.

Patrick had initially appeared startled by the music but then had begun grinning Cheshire cat-like. He was grinning so hard at the sight of Cindy and her bridesmaids' unorthodox approach toward him and Bobby-Gene that Maureen suspected his lip was stuck to his gum. She sang along to the Madge classic, which was infectiously joyous, and had her bumping hips with Donal. *You couldn't help but get into the groove*, she thought.

Just then, Noah's attention was diverted from his task, and Maureen forgot about her hip bumping as she saw his eyes bugging and his mouth drop open. What was it he'd seen? She used her hand as a sun visor again, scanning the crowd. Then she saw the culprit. A sunbather who'd sat up on her lounger to see what all the fuss was about and not bothered to put her bikini top back on. If Maureen could have lobbed something at her and shouted at her to cover herself because there was a wedding going on, she would have. But, instead, she watched as her grandson tripped over his feet, his attention finally snapping back to his ring-bearer duty. Some fancy footwork followed as he righted himself, keeping the rings on the cushion and to those not in the know, they'd think it was all part of the dance. Maureen's exhale whistled.

The song wound to a close as Cindy reached Patrick, and they both faced Bobby-Gene.

Hot and sweaty but happy the ordeal was over, Roisin, Aisling, and Moira fell into place behind the bride and groom. Noah stood at the ready with the rings.

'Welcome to you all on this special day,' Bobby-Gene began.

A cruise ship in the distance blasted its horn, drowning out the next part of the service, but some things didn't need words, and as the groom navigated his way around the bride's baby belly and planted a kiss on her lips to seal the deal an enormous cheer could be heard echoing up and down the beach.

Prologue

♥

G eorgios and Wendy waved the group of Irish guests who'd changed their lives in one short week off watching until they'd disappeared inside the airport terminal.

In the interim, Obelia pulling her case behind her, exited the ferry with a bounce in her step as she followed the steady stream of fellow passengers outside the terminal to hail a taxi. She was coming home to see her father, happy knowing that this time when she left it wouldn't be goodbye and she wouldn't be leaving her father on his own.

THE END

Thanks so much for reading The O'Maras Go Greek. If you enjoyed this latest instalment in the O'Mara family's lives please recommend the books to other readers and leave a review or starred rating on Amazon or Goodreads. I'd so appreciate it!

There are more O'Mara family shenanigans coming soon in, The Little Irish Guesthouse on the Green, Book 15, **Mrs Flaherty & the Fox**

If you'd like to ensure the Kindle edition is delivered straight to your device upon publication, pre-order is available here: https://books2 read.com/u/mgN690

About the Author

Michelle Vernal lives in Christchurch, New Zealand with her husband, two teenage sons and attention seeking tabby cats, Humphrey and Savannah. Before she started writing novels, she had a variety of jobs:

Pharmacy shop assistant, girl who sold dried up chips and sausages at a hot food stand in a British pub, girl who sold nuts (for 2 hours) on a British market stall, receptionist, P.A...Her favourite job though is the one she has now – writing stories she hopes leave her readers with a satisfied smile on their face.

Visit Michelle at www.michellevernalbooks.com to find out more about her books, and when you subscribe to her monthly newsletter, you'll receive a free O'Mara family short story to say thank you.

Also By

Novels

The Cooking School on the Bay

Second-hand Jane

Staying at Eleni's

The Traveller's Daughter

Sweet Home Summer

When We Say Goodbye

And...

Series fiction

<u>The Guesthouse on the Green Series</u>

Book 1 - O'Mara's

Book 2 – Moira-Lisa Smile

Book 3 –What goes on Tour

Book 4 – Rosi's Regrets

Book 5 – Christmas at O'Mara's

Book 6 – A Wedding at O'Mara's

Book 7 – Maureen's Song

Book 8 – The O'Maras in LaLa Land

Book 9 – Due in March

Book 10 – A Baby at O'Mara's

Book 11 – The Housewarming

Book 12 – Rainbows over O'Mara's

Book 13- An O'Maras Reunion

Book 14-The O'Maras Go Greek

Book 15 coming in January, 2024 - Mrs Flaherty & the Fox

Pre-order here: https://books2read.com/u/mgN690

Liverpool Brides Series

The Autumn Posy

The Winter Posy

The Spring Posy

The Summer Posy

Isabel's Story

The Promise

The Letter

The Little Irish Village

Christmas in the Little Irish Village

New Beginnings in the Little Irish Village

Printed in Great Britain
by Amazon